THE WAR WITH GRANDMA

Robert Kimmel Smith
and Ann Dee Ellis

DELACORTE PRESS

Text copyright © 2021 by Robert Kimmel Smith
Jacket art copyright © 2021 by Mike Heath.
Jacket images used under license from Shutterstock.com.
Map art copyright © 2021 by Sarah Hokanson

Delacorte Press is a registered trademark and the colophon is a trademark of Penguin Random House LLC.

Visit us on the Web! rhcbooks.com

Educators and librarians, for a variety of teaching tools, visit us at RHTeachersLibrarians.com

Library of Congress Cataloging-in-Publication Data
Names: Smith, Robert Kimmel, author. | Ellis, Ann Dee, author.
Title: The war with Grandma / Robert Kimmel Smith and Ann Dee Ellis.
Description: First edition. | New York : Delacorte Press, [2021] | Audience: Ages 8–12. | Audience: Grades 4–6. | Summary: When Meg finds out Grandma Sally is going to be her partner for the Centennial Strawberry Day contest, she thinks her chances at winning are gone and declares war on her grandmother.
Identifiers: LCCN 2020043219 | ISBN 9780593127469 (hardcover) | ISBN 978-0-593-31023-6 (library binding) | ISBN 978-0-593-12747-6 (ebook)
Subjects: CYAC: Grandmothers—Fiction. | Family life—Fiction. | Contests—Fiction.
Classification: LCC PZ7.S65762 Wap 2021 | DDC [Fic]—dc23

The text of this book is set in 12-point Apollo MT Pro.
Interior design by Cathy Bobak

Printed in the United States of America
10 9 8 7 6 5 4 3 2 1
First Edition

To my sweet Sammy, who keeps me on track and
is always up for an adventure. And to my mom.
I miss you every day.

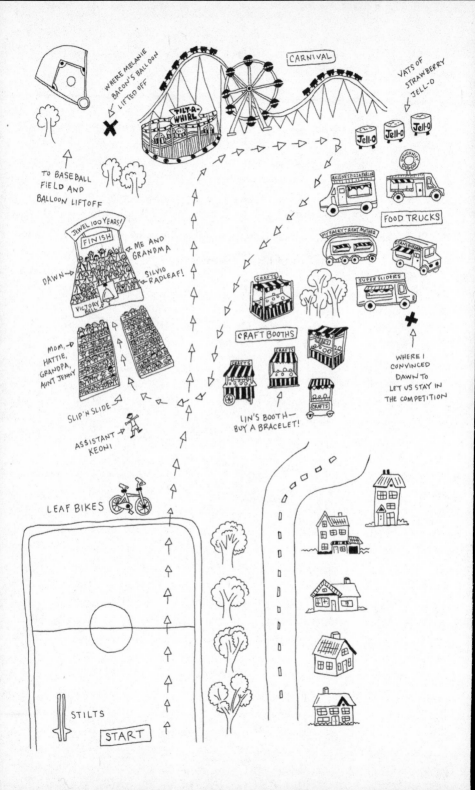

1

Meg Stokes's True Real Exposé

To Whom It May Concern:

URGENT NEWS!!!!!!!!

My grandma is ruining my life and I am so mad I can hardly breathe.

I am going to type everything that happens to me from here on out because I NEED THIS TO BE A MATTER OF PUBLIC RECORD!

This written document will not be a book or a story or an essay. It will be more like an exposé, which according to my teacher, Mr. Bailey, means a piece of writing that gets to the underbelly of things and reveals scandalous truths. So be prepared for scandal. And LOTS of it.

If you ask my dad, it all started many, many, many years ago, before I was even born. When he was in fifth grade (which is the same grade I just finished, so it *really* was forever ago), he wrote a true and real story about how his Grandpa Jack, my Great-Grandpa Jack, moved in and stole his room. His *bedroom*. So then my dad declared war on Great-Grandpa Jack, and it got ugly.

Really ugly.

Like *U-G-L-Y* ugly.

Everyone knows a room-stealing grandpa is no joke.

The fighting got so bad, my dad wrote about it for a school assignment, and then he made it into a book. *The War with Grandpa* was a pretty good true and real story. A bunch of people read it, even Great-Grandpa Jack, who said, "Peter, this is the best present ever." I don't think adults understand presents.

Dad's war was the most epic war in the history of grandkids and grandparents.

Until now.

Until today.

Until *my* war.

This exposé is about me and my sworn enemy, my archnemesis. Some call her Sally. My dad calls her Mom. My sister, Hattie, calls her Gram. The old me called her Grandma. Now I call her a *menace*. And I'm going to tell you all about her and how we're on opposing sides of this conflict. I won't leave out a single detail until there is a decisive victory by yours truly.

Things have gotten so bad that right now I am using my dad's computer.

Dad just walked in and said, "Meg, you're being ridiculous. Are you really that mad at Grandma?"

I'm not answering him. Because the answer is obviously *yes*.

I'm typing every word he says instead as a record of what happened so that all the kids in the world will remember the even more terrible War with Grandma and learn how to prepare for battle. Don't let the comfortable shoes, triangle hair, and big glasses fool you, my friends!

Dad walks over to the desk and starts distracting me again.

"What are you doing?"

"I am typing every word you say."

"Why?"

"Because I feel it's necessary."

He sits on the rocking chair he keeps in here, which is very old, like him, and looks like it's going to fall apart, like him, but it's his favorite chair. Then he clears his throat. "I'm sorry about what happened today, but I don't think it was as bad as you think it was."

That is false. It's actually worse than he thinks I think it was. I'm sure of it.

"You have to ease up," he says, looking me in the eye, so I look *him* in the eye and type at the same time. I will not be intimidated.

"I'm never going to ease up, Dad."

"Meg, this has gone too far."

"I don't know what you mean."

"I mean, can you give your grandmother a break?"

"No."

"Or at least give *me* a break?"

"No."

"Megan, please, stop typing."

"I'm sorry, Dad, I can't stop typing, but I can tell you that my feelings have surpassed anger. I am currently furious. Vehement. Incensed!" I've been using the online thesaurus because Dad keeps it as his home page and the word of the day is always *right there*. "I need to find a new partner." There, I said it at last.

Dad heaves an enormous tired sigh, which makes me feel bad but not that bad.

"Meg. You can't get a new partner and you know it."

And here's the whole heart of the matter. I am in a competition (more on that later) where I will, **I WILL,** win the prize of my dreams. The prize of my happiness and freedom! I know I can do it. I know **I WILL** do it. The only thing holding me back—the only *person* holding me back—is my "partner." She is sabotaging me.

SABOTAGING!

And no one even cares! No one!

They're all acting like the events of today are *acceptable*!

I try to compose myself. I say in my most serious voice, "Dad. Grandma and I have come to a crossroads."

"A crossroads?"

I say nothing because I don't know exactly what a crossroads is.

Then my dear old dad stands up and says, "Can you really type that fast?"

"I can."

"How?"

"Typing club."

"Typing club? You're really, really fast."

"Dad, I'm not even the fastest. I'm fourth."

"Who's the fastest?"

"Diego Martinez, and I don't want to talk about him."

"Well, you're faster than me." For the first time since he started talking, I actually agree with him.

"Thank you."

"Will you go down and at least talk to her?"

"Who?"

"You know who."

"I do not know to whom you are referring."

"Grandma Sally."

"You mean the person stomping all over my hopes and dreams?"

"Meg. Come on."

And then I start to fume and I billow up in even more anger.

"Fume? Billow up?" Dad says, reading over my shoulder.

That's growing annoying, so I say in a very loud voice: "Yes. Fume. Billow up, Dad. Billow up in anger like a tsunami! You were at the competition today! You *saw* what happened! I have every right to billow up." I pause and then I say, I say it right to his face, I say, "Grandma Sally and I are at war."

Dad closes his mouth and acts like he's being normal, but he's not being normal. His face gets red and he starts to giggle. GIGGLE!

"It's not funny, Dad!"

"I know. I know, it's not," he chokes out.

"It's *really* not funny."

"I know."

And that's where we are, people. That's where we are. My dad, laughing at me. LAUGHING. My grandma, downstairs, making a mockery of my pain.

So let it go on official record: I am not typing this because I want to be a writer like my dad. I'm not typing this because of some school assignment. I'm not even typing this because I need to "cope with my feelings," like my Aunt Jenny is always saying (because she's a therapist and one time made me lie on my back and breathe through my nose and think about dogs running through waves at the beach and it really does help—I highly recommend it).

The reason I am typing this is to make a record of this war with my grandma, because if I don't, no one will believe me.

No one believes kids at all, actually.

And Dad should know.

Because here's the thing, and I hate to say it: history is repeating itself. It really is, but way, way worse, because mistakes have been forgotten.

And now I am in a war.

And this time, the kid is going to win!

2

How It All Started

It all started on a beautiful, sunny day in May. The last day of school, in fact. I was minding my own business cleaning out my desk, organizing my backpack, and thinking about summer break.

I was both happy and sad the school year was over. I was happy because, well, duh, freedom for three months. I was sad because Lin, my best friend, lives far far far away from me. Actually, everyone lives far away from me, because our house is way outside town, a twenty-minute drive by the lake, on a dirt road where nobody goes unless they're lost or delivering bills or dentist birthday postcards.

We live there because Dad quit his job to be a full-time writer and Mom thought we should "simplify our lives," which I know really means writers aren't as rich as they look. They found this tiny house where the closest

8

neighbors are Mrs. Jensen's brown horses, which isn't *all* bad. I've had some deep conversations with those horses. They're great listeners.

Dad loves the house because he says it has clean lines that Great-Grandpa Jack would have appreciated. Great-Grandpa Jack was an architect. Dad also says it's perfect for a writer because it's quiet and private and secluded.

Perfect for him.

Not so perfect for me and my sister, Hattie.

There are zero kids.

Zero.

In Lin's neighborhood, up on the east side, where most people live and where the library and the park and the big grocery store are, they have block parties, ride bikes to the gas station for frozen lemonades, and play night games. Summertime is one huge party.

Out here where we live, we eat hundreds of peanut butter sandwiches, dig holes in the mud, and play kickball with the horses. Summertime is one huge snore.

Now you might say, *Meg, what's the big deal?*

Ride the bus over there.

Get your parents to drive you to your friend's house.

Walk on your own two legs.

And I'd say, I know. I would but first of all, the city buses do not come near our house. The school bus does, but that stops once school stops.

And second of all, my mom's work is forty miles away

at a software company in a neighboring town and we only have one car. My dad has to walk to his part-time job at town hall. It's mostly uphill, so it takes him AN HOUR to get there.

Lin lives *even farther* away than the government offices. This all means if I want to hang out with my friends, I have to walk across the country to get to their houses.

This is the worst, because (a) I'm not that cardiovascularly fit, if you want to know the truth, though I can do the wall sit for forty-eight seconds. Time yourself and see how hard that is. Diego knows, because he could do it for forty-three seconds. And (b) I'd have to take my sister Hattie with me, which makes the walk that much longer and sometimes when she gets tired, she sits in the middle of the road. She really does.

So I was contemplating the boringness of the next few months when Mr. Bailey made the most important announcement of my life.

"I have some handouts for everyone," he said. "The summer reading program list has been finalized. Basketball camp at the high school. Chess club put on by Mrs. Whatcott." He held up a flyer for each one.

Same old, same old.

Then he said, "This last one is a contest that's happening during Strawberry Days." He looked at it more closely. "Huh. It's specifically for incoming sixth graders." He looked at us. "It's for you guys."

Strawberry Days? A contest? For sixth graders?

"What kind of contest?" Diego said.

Diego and I have a long history with contests. I leaned forward so I could make sure I didn't miss anything.

"Read the flyer yourself," Mr. Bailey said. "We have a lot to get through today."

My heart raced.

Strawberry Days is the best time of the year, hands down.

Our town puts on the festival every summer to honor our history of being one of the biggest strawberry growers in the United States. We don't have many strawberry fields anymore, but we still celebrate. We have a huge strawberry pancake breakfast and a carnival with rides and performances and a farmer's market and fireworks. There's always strawberry contests, and once there was a guy who got shot out of a cannon into a pool of strawberry jam. Everyone lives for Strawberry Days.

To up the suspense, Mr. Bailey, instead of handing out the flyers, started talking about how proud he was of us and how he was going to miss us. I really liked Mr. Bailey because he didn't treat us like four-year-olds. He let us make a trebuchet for the medieval festival and we got to launch eggs at each other as practice, and my egg splattered all over Diego and his friends Leroy and Eli, who were in the target zone making faces.

Finally, after his long speech, he gave us the flyers and I went right to the red one.

The town of Jewel is proud to present

THE STRAWBERRY AMBASSADOR COMPETITION

In honor of the Strawberry Days Centennial Celebration
WEDNESDAY, JUNE 11—SATURDAY, JUNE 14

We invite all Jewel County incoming sixth-grade
students to compete in a series of challenges.
Each student will raise money for a charity of
their choosing.
The top fundraising student will be named
THE STRAWBERRY AMBASSADOR!
The winner will enjoy an honorary title and plaque
declaring them as kid ambassador for the town and
will receive two Leaf electric cargo bikes.
To enter, students must submit a six-page essay
about what makes the town of Jewel great.
The writers of the top five essays will be chosen as
participants in the challenges.

ENTER BY SATURDAY, JUNE 7, 9:00 A.M.
Sponsored by Leaf Bikes, Soelberg Grocery,
Knudsen Strawberry Farms, the Jewel Restaurant
Alliance and Milo's Sporting Goods.

* ALL SELECTED PARTICIPANTS MUST BE PARTNERED
WITH A PARENT/GUARDIAN/RESPONSIBLE ADULT.

Holding the flyer, I felt woozy.

Like my legs got shaky and I saw dots floating in front of my eyes.

"What's wrong?" Lin asked. She was waving a hand in front of me. "You look like a dead fish."

"Have you seen a dead fish?"

"Yes," she said. "A rotten dead fish, too."

Normally this kind of comment would make me mad because I don't love to look like rotten dead fish, but I probably did look like a rotten dead fish because I was in shock.

I held up the flyer. "Did you read this?"

"Not yet. Why?"

I took a deep breath and said, "Lin. This is the most important thing that has ever happened to me."

She took it from me and read it and I tried to be calm by thinking about dogs running through waves in the ocean.

"Oh my gosh," she gasped. "Oh my gosh!"

I grabbed her shoulders and shook her.

"Leaf electric cargo bikes, Lin! Leaf electric cargo bikes!"

I had been drooling over Leaf electric cargo bikes ever since Mr. Bailey showed us a TED Talk by the guy who invented them, Silvio Radleaf. He was actually from our town! And the bikes were amazing. They were fast, they could go for miles without being charged, and there was room in the cargo bags to carry practically your whole house. "I could

13

ride to your neighborhood. I wouldn't even have to pedal!" I said to Lin.

Someone threw a paper airplane at my head, but I didn't care.

"We could hang out every single day!" Lin cried. And then she said, "But I think you have to pedal."

"You know what I mean! I could meet you at the pool. The library. The movies. Do you realize how this would change *everything*?"

"Oh my gosh," she kept saying, and I kept shaking her.

"What about the essay?" she asked.

"What *about* the essay?" I answered. "I don't care if I have to write a hundred pages. I'm getting those bikes."

Lin hates writing things. She one time talked Mr. Bailey into letting her do a dance performance with a one-page explanation instead of writing a five-page paper about King Tutankhamen. Lin has been in dance classes since she was three, and I really felt like I got to know King Tut in a new way through her performance. Everyone said that.

I, on the other hand, love writing. Clearly. But also, at the Writers' Olympics, I tied EVERY YEAR with the same person for first place.

Diego.

I looked at Diego and he looked at me.

Diego lived by Lin and already had a pretty sweet

mountain bike, but I knew he'd want to win the competition. And we both knew it wasn't going to be pretty.

"Let the games begin," he called.

Lin said, "Oh please."

But I said right back, "Yes. They've already begun."

While I was getting my certificate for completing fifth grade, I thought about all the things I needed to do to prepare.

First of all, the essay. I already had ideas of what I could write about: facts about the town, strawberry mythology, my own personal relationship with aggregate fruit.

Second, I felt like I needed to get in better shape and train, because what if the challenges were super athletic and you had to carry a basket of strawberries for ten miles or something? Like I said, I'm not the most fit person on the earth and I mostly walk home from the school bus stop for exercise and it was fine because really, how often do you have to run a mile? In PE it's once a year, but they let you walk it as long as you finish before the period is up.

I was worried.

And finally, I had to solidify my partner.

This was a no-brainer. Dad would for sure be my partner, because he and I are very competitive and both like to put money toward good causes like the holiday toy drive, so fundraising would be easy.

Also, Dad loves Strawberry Days. One time he ate four buckets of strawberries at the carnival to win a twenty-five-dollar gift card to Dolly's Diner. He was up against Billy Hogwater, who is the strongest man I've ever seen—he once lifted a car all by himself.

Everyone thought Billy would win for sure, because my dad is very wiry and wears glasses (not that wearing glasses means you can't eat a lot of strawberries, but you know, he doesn't look like the kind of person who could shovel it in). But Dad—you should have seen it—Dad was stuffing handfuls of strawberries in his mouth, juice dripping down his white shirt, and Mom kept saying, "Oh my. Oh my. Peter. Slow down!" But me and Hattie were screaming, "Keep going, Dad! You can do it!" And he did not slow down. NO, HE DID NOT! He won big-time! He was covered in strawberries and tears were streaming down his face and I'd never been so proud.

He was in the bathroom for hours when we got home, but he won and he said he didn't regret it one bit.

This is all to say, Dad had to be my partner and we'd be unstoppable.

Everything seemed so simple back then. The world was bright and the future seemed sure. I was beginning my journey to Leaf electric bike freedom.

Little did I know how fast brightness can turn to darkness.

Little did I know that futures are unknown and treacherous.

Little did I know that the essay, the exercise, all the preparation, those things were nothing.

In a competition like this your partner is the thing that will make or break you. Your partner is the key to victory.

And little did I know I would be forced, FORCED to work with the one person I would never have chosen.

Not because I don't love her. I love her very much.

And not because she's a bad person. She's actually one of the best.

In fact, before all this went down, she was pretty close to my favorite person ever.

But let it be known to all people all over the world: **my Grandma Sally is the worst Strawberry Days partner in the history of the world.**

I don't feel bad writing that bolded in black ink in this official exposé that I plan to send to every single person who does or does not have an address.

3

The Long Walk Home

After school on that fateful day, Hattie and I took the school bus home. I still remember it like it was yesterday. Everything was a bit more special than usual. The birds were chirping. The sky was clear. Our bus driver, Judy, who is grumpy and has a barrette with eyes on it that she clips on the back of her head and tells us she's watching us, she wasn't wearing the barrette that day and she even said "Hello, girls!" when we got on.

We got the seat where the bus window actually works so we had fresh air. And the kid Tony who gets off at our stop and likes to sit behind us and make loud noises and kick our seat wasn't on the bus. It was like the universe was smiling down on me.

Once we were off the bus, we started the long walk to our house.

I was supposed to go to an end-of-school party at a girl named Raven's house, but Lin wasn't going to be there because her family was going camping and I was too anxious about the competition. I wanted to go home and think about it and maybe start on my essay.

"Can I ride the other bike if you win?" Hattie asked. She was wearing a pink shirt that said CHANGE THE WORLD and orange shorts with rainbow shoes. She looked like a bag of jelly beans. I, on the other hand, was wearing a black T-shirt and jeans shorts, which was basically the uniform for fifth graders.

"You can ride the other bike if I give permission," I said.

"What?" she said. "Permission?"

"Yes. Permission."

Here's the thing, Hattie would get plenty of chances to ride, but I knew it wouldn't just be her who would be asking to borrow it. I felt like order should be established because maybe Lin would be dropped off at our house and we'd want to ride together, or Dad might want to take it to work instead of walking, and maybe Mom would want to use it to visit her friends in town. I thought about making a bike chart so people could sign up to use it. Maybe they could even pay me! Or do my chores or give me things in exchange for bike time. With two Leaf bikes, my life was going to completely change.

"But if I help you, I think I should get the other bike."

"How are you going to help me?"

"I-I-I'll have water for you and bring you snacks during the competitions. I'll make posters and signs."

"You have to do that anyway because you're my sister."

"No, I don't."

"Yes, you do."

"Uh, no I don't."

And then I reminded Hattie how she helped me with my campaign to be fifth-grade mayor for Junior Achievement City and we had buttons that said *I SHOULDN'T HAVE TO BEG, VOTE FOR MEG.* We made like a hundred and we also made sugar cookies with my face on them and they didn't actually look like me but we tried and Hattie was all about it. I didn't have to give her anything.

"Remember that?"

"Yeah. It was super nice of me. You should give me the other bike just for that!" she said.

"But I lost, so was that really helping or hurting?"

Then Hattie got mad and we got in an argument and it was supposed to be the best day, so I finally said, "Fine. You can use the other bike almost whenever you want unless I need it for something else."

"Fine," she said, and then we kept walking, except with her stomping a little bit ahead of me. Sometimes Hattie can be so annoying.

We passed the old farmhouse that was haunted and then crossed the empty lot. "So what charity would you pick?" Hattie asked because she couldn't stand not talking for more than two minutes.

I kicked a rock. "For sure the Alzheimer's Association."

She nodded. "That's what I thought you'd pick. Grandma Sally and Dad will be happy."

I chose the Alzheimer's Association because it's how my Great-Grandpa Jack died. My Great-Grandpa Jack was my dad's mom's dad. He loved to fish. He also was in World War Two before he and my great-grandma got married and had my Grandma Sally. He lived with Grandma Sally and Grandpa Arthur after my great-grandma died and that's when the other legendary war, the war with my dad, got started.

Great-Grandpa Jack ended up living at my dad's house for ten years! And he and my dad were best friends pretty much until he died. I didn't show up until later and Hattie even later than that, so our family tree is big.

Dad talks about him all the time and he takes us fishing whenever he's feeling sad about Great-Grandpa Jack because they used to go together. Dad has told us a billion times not to use tuna as bait because it scares the fish away. That was apparently a Great-Grandpa Jack tip, and I don't blame the fish.

One time we went to a 5K that was four hours away to help raise money for the Alzheimer's Association. It was really fun because there were hundreds of people, including my Grandma Sally and my Grandpa Arthur. We wore shirts with Grandpa Jack's face on them and walked and held pinwheels along with a bunch of other people. At the end we got medals. Dad was crying a little.

I was thinking about the 5K when Hattie and I passed Trudy Martin's house, which is a trailer that she's painted to look like a submarine. She collects all kinds of cool things like metal ducks and spinning flowers and a sculpture of an armadillo. She also owns a food truck called My Fairy Treat Mother and sells the best candy in the state.

"Hey, Trudy," I said. She was pulling weeds.

"You girls are out early. You staying out of trouble?" she called, kneeling back and wiping her forehead. She had her hair tied up in a bandana and was wearing overalls.

"Yup," I said.

"Last day of school." Hattie smiled.

"Is that so?" Trudy said, and then she asked, "You all want some taffy to celebrate?"

"Yes!" we cheered, and ran over.

Once Trudy showed me how to make banana taffy, and it's hard. You have to get everything just right, not only the ingredients but the timing and the temperature. It's complicated but so worth it, and Trudy offering it now made the day all the more special.

"I'll give you an assortment," Trudy said as she loaded up a bag for us—Fruity Pebble flavor included.

"This is bigger than my head," Hattie said, in awe.

"Thanks, Trudy!" I said, putting the bag into my backpack for safekeeping from Hattie.

"Enough to last for the summer." Trudy winked.

This really was the best day.

4

Roger Rabbit

Me and Hattie decided to decorate the house in honor of the competition and make hamburgers and french fries and our special cabbage salad as a celebration, which for Hattie may have been more because of the last day of school or the huge bag of taffy, it's a toss-up. But for me it was definitely because I knew I was going to compete in and win the Strawberry Ambassador Competition.

Also, we love to cook together. We make dinner all the time. One time we copied the recipes of an entire season of our favorite show, *Amateur Kid Chef*. We had to stop after that because Dad said we couldn't buy a new spice at the market every trip, but we did eat pretty great for a while.

We worked the whole afternoon to make it perfect and

I did some good essay brainstorming in the process. When I saw Dad coming down the driveway, I ran out to meet him and said, "Dad! I have something very important to tell you."

I was jumping up and down at that point, and Hattie was playing her trumpet from the front porch like we planned.

"Okay, okay," he laughed. "Calm down. Can we eat first?"

"Fine, but hurry," I said, and dragged him to the house.

"Did you tell him?" Hattie asked, completely out of breath.

"He wants to eat first," I explained. Mom had to work late, so it would just be us.

We sat down at the kitchen table, surrounded by hanging paper strawberries that me and Hattie had drawn. I poured him our special strawberry lemonade that we made using frozen strawberries we found in the freezer and half a lemon because that's all we had, so it was mostly sugar water with mushy strawberries floating on top but it still tasted good.

We also made paper place mats with Leaf cargo bikes drawn on them and I wrote down all the stats on the side.

They can go twenty-eight miles an hour!

They come in three different colors!

The cargo bags hold as much as twenty-two house bricks! (We have bricks in our backyard for an outdoor fireplace Mom and Dad were going to make someday, and so me and Hattie ran out in the middle of decorating and stacked them up as a test and Hattie said, "Whoa, that *is* a ton," and it really was!)

Zero emissions!

Save the earth!

Easy to fix!

"Wow," Dad said. "This is fancy. Happy last day of school, you two. How was the dance festival?"

What?

Didn't he see the hanging strawberries?

Wasn't he enjoying his delicious strawberry drink?

Wasn't he at all curious about my important news?

But no, he was asking about the dance festival.

We always have a dance festival at the end of school, which I don't love. Hattie started telling him about the second-grade jungle dance and how her friend Erin was in her dance spot at the beginning and she didn't know why but she had to just go to Erin's spot and that messed her up but she did it anyway and she thought it turned out pretty good.

They kept talking and talking and talking about I don't know what! I really don't know because none of this was important! Not one thing they were saying mattered and I was about to burst! And I did burst!

"STOOOOOOP!" I yelled as loud as I could.

Dad looked at me.

Hattie looked at me.

"Meg, my dear, let's not raise our voices at the table," he said.

"Sorry," I said, trying to calm down. "I'm very sorry it's just that"—I glanced at Hattie—"as I mentioned to you earlier, I have some *very important* news, even more important than the end-of-school dance festival, which happens every year, but this news, this has never happened before and I really want to tell you about it and if you look around, you will see that it's about Strawberry Days."

Dad smiled.

"Do you already know?"

He nodded, taking a bite of burger. "I do."

"About the Strawberry Ambassador Competition?"

He nodded.

"Why didn't you tell me?!"

He put a finger up because he was chewing. "I just found out today," he finally said.

"Really?"

"I'm a lowly clerk, they don't tell me things."

"Dad!" I cried. "Can you believe it? This is everything! This is the best thing that has ever happened to me. We have to win. We have to."

And then I was the one who couldn't stop talking. I really couldn't.

"We must start preparing. Diego is for sure going to do it. He's always out to get me, and he can't win, Dad. You know he can't win."

Dad agreed.

I kept going. "I wonder why it's just sixth graders? And how will they judge? Are they using judges? Do you know what the challenges are going to be?"

"Nope," Dad said.

Ugh. I took a bite of burger and kept talking. "You've seen the bikes, though, right? They are so amazing. Me and Hattie saw a video about a lady who rode one all the way from Maine to Alaska! She had her guinea pig in the basket with her." We'd managed to do a bit of research amid preparing for Dad to get home.

"No," Hattie said. "That was a dog."

"It was?"

"Yeah. You thought that was a guinea pig?"

"Well, whatever. Maybe we could ride them to Prince Edward Island!" The thought just popped into my head. I've always wanted to go where *Anne of Green Gables* was set and right then I knew I'd ride there, even if it was thousands of miles away. With an electric bike the whole world was my oyster. I'd ride there, my hair blowing in the wind, the ocean salt spraying on my face, maybe our cat Daisy in the basket like that lady in the video.

Hattie said, "It's an island. You can't ride a bike to an island."

Then me and Hattie got in another argument and I couldn't hear what she was saying over my voice talking over her until Dad broke it up by clapping like a sea otter.

We both went silent.

"I have some bad news." Dad sat back and looked at the ceiling.

He had bad news? About the competition? About Prince Edward Island? We didn't have to go to Prince Edward Island. It was just an idea.

"I'm so sorry, Meg," he said.

I looked at Hattie. She looked at me.

"It's just that . . ." He closed his eyes. "I feel so bad . . ." He covered his face. Was he crying? "I feel so bad . . . for your friend Diego and how he will *feel* when we CRUSH this competition and we *will* ride those bikes wherever we want. We are going to be unbeatable!"

He jumped up and started doing the Roger Rabbit, which is an old dance move that my dad used to do in high school. Usually it's pretty embarrassing and I encourage him to never ever do it, but that night, with the Strawberry Ambassador Competition win pretty much our destiny, it was the most beautiful Roger Rabbit I had ever seen. Hattie and I joined in and we all danced the night away.

5

Grandma Sally

I now interrupt the Roger Rabbit Strawberry Celebration to discuss a pressing matter. Some of you may be thinking, What about the grandma? What about the menace? Isn't she your partner? Isn't she the subject of this very well-crafted exposé?

Don't worry, all will be explained in due time.

Grandma had not entered the picture the night of our party. But looking back, I sometimes wonder if she had some kind of supernatural idea that it was coming, that *she* was coming.

In fact, sometimes I wonder what she was doing the night we were drinking delicious strawberry lemonade, daydreaming of riding bikes to islands, and dancing our faces off. Was she eating tomato corn chip sandwiches (her favorite) and planning my demise? Was she sitting in a bathtub (she makes her own bath bombs) laughing at our delight? Was she practicing a solo (alto but sometimes second soprano) about ruining children's lives?

I mean, technically she had no idea there was such a thing as a Strawberry Ambassador Competition at that time, but that doesn't matter. I still choose to think she had some kind of foresight, some kind of idea, that she was about to do something major to interfere with my happiness.

So before I go any further, it's very important for you, dear reader, to get a clear understanding of my grandmother and some of the changes (she might call them "evolutions") she's been going through so that when infiltration and sabotage happens later—not much later, mind you; our celebration was very short-lived—you will understand what I was dealing with.

First of all, as mentioned, Grandma Sally is married to my Grandpa Arthur, who is an accountant who hasn't retired yet because he loves working with numbers, helping people, and wearing bow ties. He looks just like my dad except he has a mustache that he combs and puts oil on. He also likes reading the newspaper (the actual newspaper!) and he enjoys putting ketchup on all food, including mashed potatoes, corn, turkey sandwiches, and macaroni and cheese. It's very disturbing but that's a topic for another day.

That's Grandpa Arthur. I love him very much and he

always gives us black licorice, which is delicious and Hattie hates it so I get all of hers.

I also love Grandma Sally, aka the enemy, who never gives us black licorice. She's a chocolate lover.

Once upon a time Grandma Sally was like other grandmas. Along with Grandpa Arthur, she raised my dad and his sister Jenny, both at home and at school because she taught Family and Consumer Sciences at the local high school.

People say she was an excellent teacher even though she gave my dad a C in her class because he kept not getting up in the middle of the night to feed a fake baby she made everyone take care of to see if they were going to be good parents.

Grandma did so well at teaching that she won the Golden Apple and Teacher of the Year before she retired.

She then took care of Great-Grandpa Jack until he died. Dad is proud of her, despite his not-so-good grades, and he's actually a pretty good dad so her fake baby test was unfair, I think.

We go visit Grandma Sally and Grandpa Arthur a few times a year.

When we are there, we usually go swimming, paint mugs, and make root beer floats.

One time she helped us learn how to sew shorts with whatever cloth we picked out at the store. Hattie chose the weirdest fabric with floating cupcakes and unicorn heads.

We'd do puzzles and play charades (Grandma could do the best Dog Man) and she'd read us stories, so many stories.

Pretty normal Grandma stuff.

No problems.

Everything fine.

Expected.

Then, a little after Grandma retired from teaching, the "evolutions" started.

I will number them for organizational purposes.

EVOLUTION #1:
She dyed her white hair purple.

Like bright purple.

Like grape soda purple.

Some might say, "Who cares? I dyed my hair pink yesterday."

And I'd say, "Yes. I like pink hair and turquoise hair and blue hair. In fact, one day Lin and I hope to dye her hair rainbow."

The issue here is when Dad saw her for the first time with her soda hair, he froze.

"What's wrong?" Grandma asked, smiling. She had never ever done anything remotely colorful with her hair. Ever. "You like my new look?"

"When did you do that?" He dropped his suitcase.

"Oh, just trying something new. Did you know you can

dye your hair using Kool-Aid? I've been doing research. You can also use sage or carrot juice or even coffee!"

Dad stared at her. "You did that with Kool-Aid?"

"Yup. I love it and can't wait to run more tests."

After that trip, Dad told us we could not copy any of those kinds of science experiments.

EVOLUTION #2:
She gave up the living room couch.

The next time we were over, Grandma had red hair— beet juice dyed, she let us know—and when we walked into the house, we got another surprise . . . there was a trampoline! It had replaced the living room couch! It was a small one, but still!

"What in the world, Mom?" Dad said.

Hattie and I screamed. We ran and jumped on it immediately, as anyone would. Dad was dumbfounded. "You got a trampoline? Aren't they bad for people in your, errr, condition?"

"What did you just say? My condition? You mean my *age*?"

Dad flushed. Grandma did not like comments about her age. I could relate—having a birthday that came late in the year used to mean kids would call me a baby. It's not like you had any say about how old you were.

"Come on, Mom, you know what I mean. We never had a trampoline growing up. You said they were dangerous and didn't you say you wanted to go easy on your right ankle? The one you hurt as a kid?"

"Did I say that?"

"Yes, Mom, you did," Dad said emphatically.

"Huh," she said. "That's odd. Either you heard wrong or I was misinformed, because first of all, they are safe. Second of all, they are excellent for your health. They help with circulation, digestion, and elimination and boost brain function."

Elimination? Gross. I made a face at Hattie, who made a face back.

"And third of all, I bought *trampolines,* plural." Grandma smiled.

"There are more?!" I said.

Hattie and I stopped jumping.

"Yes. I found them at a yard sale and they were practically free, right, Arthur?"

Grandpa Arthur was sitting in his recliner watching us jump. "They were a dollar each, so not free."

"Where are the other ones?" Dad asked, sounding more alarmed than excited.

"Try the kitchen, the bedroom, there's even one in the bathroom," Grandpa said. He didn't seem too excited either, more bored really.

"But why?" Dad asked Grandma.

"Your dad hasn't been as enthusiastic about exercise lately, so I thought I'd put them where he could see them and maybe when he was walking by he might take a jump."

"Not likely," Grandpa Arthur said.

Grandma gave Grandpa a look.

Dad gave Grandma a different look.

And I gave Hattie a very, very different look before we each raced off throughout the house with Dad yelling after us to be careful.

EVOLUTION #3:
She decided she wanted to go flying.

The last summer we went to visit and rather than watch movies and eat popcorn, Grandma had us make dream boards.

"Dream boards? What's a dream board?" Dad asked.

"Dream boards are where you cut out pictures and words that show how you envision your future, who you want to be, what you want to do," Grandma said.

"Are you serious?" Dad said.

Mom elbowed Dad. Then she said, "I think it sounds wonderful, Sally."

"Thank you for that, Stephanie," Grandma said. "We can't all be sticks in the mud, can we?" Then she said, "Come see!"

In Grandma's bedroom it was a dream board explosion. They were all over the place. Like every wall was plastered with Grandma's dreams, and wow, were they big.

There were pictures of rock climbers and magicians and skydivers. Pictures of artists and builders and scuba divers. Pictures of puppies and beaches and famous actors.

There were also words from magazines glued all over the pictures. *LIVE LIFE! GO BIG! DARE! WONDER! EXPLORE!* And Grandma's favorite saying that she made up, I think, was painted huge over the bedroom door: *GO BOLD OR GO OLD!*

"What is going on?" Dad said. Poor Dad.

"Your grandmother is redecorating," Grandpa Arthur said. He leaned against the wall, almost dislodging a dream board on travel destinations. "She's discovering her inner self."

"Is that what I'm doing?" Grandma said. I couldn't tell if she was mad or not.

He smiled. "What would you call it?"

Grandma put a hand on her hip. "I'm figuring out what I want to do next, is all. I think it's helpful for everyone to think about those kinds of things. Your grandpa is busy at work and I'm busy doing this." She gestured to the walls.

All of us were kind of overwhelmed. I mean, as I said before, not only had Grandma had the same hairstyle for years and years, she also wore the same jeans, the same shirts, the same shoes. She'd lived in the same house, drove the same car, and ate the same muffins since we were born.

Now we were standing in her dream room.

"You want to jump out of a plane, Mom?" Dad asked, staring at a picture of a person hanging from a striped parachute in the sky.

She folded her arms. "I do, Peter. I really do. And I've met some ladies who I might do it with since your father has no interest."

Dad looked at Grandpa Arthur, who seemed older than usual. "She has an adventure group now," Grandpa said.

Dad turned to Grandma Sally.

"Yup. It's fantastic. Women of all walks of life and it's really opening my eyes to the possibilities. We're going to learn to belly dance."

Dad went pale. I wasn't sure why that was so bad. I thought the trampoline in the bathroom was way weirder but also very awesome.

"And I'm trying out for a play!" Grandma said.

Dad had to sit down. Grandpa Arthur rubbed his shoulders. "You're going to be amazing, Sally," Grandpa said. "Isn't she, Peter?"

Dad sighed. Then he said, "Yeah, Mom. I'm sure you will be."

We all came home with posters of our dreams, but Dad

told us he wouldn't sign a release to let us go skydiving and not to bother to ask.

FINAL EVOLUTION:
Grandma is going to become famous.

It was that Christmas where, instead of staying at home, we drove eight hours to see Grandma in *A Christmas Carol*.

She was the Ghost of Christmas Future, which personally is my favorite ghost if you want to know the truth, and she had no lines but it didn't matter. She was so good! Like the creepiest Ghost of Christmas Future I had ever seen. She wore a huge mask and a big old black cloak and walked around on stilts so she could tower over Ebenezer Scrooge.

Grandma told us she'd practiced for hours to make sure she didn't fall. Then she gave us all stilts as gifts!

On the car ride home, I heard Dad say to my mom that it was an old-life crisis.

"That's not a thing," Mom laughed.

"I think it is," Dad said. "She went skydiving, Steph. You don't go skydiving when you're almost seventy."

"Why are you so upset about this? She's having fun," Mom said.

Dad sighed. "I don't know. It's just, I don't know."

At first I agreed with Mom. Why was Dad so upset

about Grandma trying new things? Then I thought I might be scared if Dad or Mom started jumping out of planes or started belly dancing without telling me. You come to expect people to be a certain way and when they suddenly change, it can be hard.

This is all to say my Grandma Sally was going bold instead of old and, in a lot of ways, it was great for me and Hattie. We liked seeing what was going to happen next. She was trying out to be Miss Hannigan from the musical *Annie* for her next play, which is a plum part, she told us. PLUM.

"This will be my breakout role. Mark my words," she said to us over the phone. "Wait until I get in the movies, girls. I'll bring you out to Hollywood."

Who wouldn't want to go to Hollywood?

No skin off my nose, as Grandma used to say.

None at all.

Until . . . until there *was* skin off my nose. *Way* too much skin off my nose, and it was coming right around the corner. Fasten your seatbelts.

6

Shipshape

But before Grandma Sally comes in, I had to get shipshape.

For two weeks I worked on my essay. I walked to the lake and threw rocks in because sometimes that helps me brainstorm. I wrote it in pencil first. Then again in pen. Then I wrote it on the computer, draft after draft, trying to get it just right.

In the meantime I wrote Dad notes like **WE CAN DO THIS!** and **THERE IS NO I IN TEAM** and **ALONE WE CAN DO LITTLE, TOGETHER WE CAN DO SO MUCH.** I found that one online and it's by Helen Keller. I think it's really good. I left the notes in his office and in his walking shoes and in the bathroom.

Dad said they were helping.

"Are they really?"

"They are. I gotta say. They're motivating."

He left me notes back.

STAY STRAWBERRY! Or **THEY CAN'T TAKE US DOWN, THEY CAN ONLY HURT US BERRY MUCH!** Or **WE ARE THE (STRAWBERRY) CHOMPIONS!**

We did sit-ups and push-ups. We memorized the most recent census of the town. Dad made a huge poster with a list of all the past mayors of Jewel and the members of the school board and town council.

"Why are you doing all this?" Mom asked after work one night.

"Steph. We have to be prepared. They could have a town trivia game."

"Yeah, Mom," I said. Dad and I had made a list of possible events, and trivia seemed like a no-brainer.

We learned the town song.

We watched videos of past Strawberry Days.

While Dad was working, I made Hattie walk to the Biddulph Insurance Office with me the week before the competition, to ask Frank Biddulph, who used to be on the town council, if he knew any details. Frank and my dad were friends. Frank always wore a suit and tie and red suspenders, even when he went fishing or to a dirt bike race or horseback riding.

He used to be in charge of all the town events like Strawberry Days and the Trunk or Treat and the Holiday Village and the Dropping of the Jewel on New Year's Eve. He was very strict about rule keeping, according to my dad, who said Frank got a kid disqualified from the Easter coloring contest for using markers instead of crayons. Now Frank was just a regular citizen.

But a regular citizen who usually had good information.

"I know nothing," Frank said.

"Nothing?"

"Nothing."

"But you know everything," I said, and he laughed.

"Not anymore," he said. "Haven't you learned that yet?"

I shifted in my chair.

"But, like, if you were to guess, do you think the challenges would be more physical or mental?"

Frank leaned back and folded his arms on his belly. His goatee looked itchy.

"If I were to guess, and it would be a guess, I have nothing to do with this, you hear me?"

"I hear you," I said.

He looked at Hattie.

"I hear you," Hattie said.

He seemed satisfied with that. "If I were to guess, I'd say both."

"Both physical and mental?"

"Yup." He nodded. "And emotional and spiritual."

"Spiritual?"

"Spiritual."

I flared my nostrils to let him know I knew he was toying with me.

We were sitting in his office, which was a small room with no windows and lots of posters of cats and dogs. My thighs kept sticking together and Hattie was fanning herself with a life insurance pamphlet.

"Is it going to be hard?" Hattie asked.

"Oh, it's going to be extremely difficult," Frank said. "They've never done anything like this in the history of Jewel and you know Dawn Allerton is in charge."

I coughed to hide my alarm.

Dawn Allerton was the president of the town council and she was an attorney with a huge brick building downtown. She had a reputation of being the toughest person in the county for a lot of different reasons—there were billboards of her face all over the highway that said HIRE DAWN! SHE'S THE ONE!, and she even used self-defense to catch a robber at the grocery store and held him there until the police showed up. She spoke at our elementary school last year. It was the first time in the history of Wasatch Elementary that no one, not one kid, made a sound. She's that powerful.

I looked up to her in a lot of ways.

"Do you think that's bad news?" I asked.

He shrugged. "I don't think it's bad at all. She's incredibly no-nonsense and she'll run things like a ship."

"Like a ship?" Hattie said.

Frank nodded. "You ever heard of shipshape, Hattie?"

"Nope."

"It means everything will be in order. On a seafaring vessel, there can be nothing amiss. Everything has to be in its proper place, perfect, precise. I'm guessing this competition will be shipshape, not for the fainthearted."

I nodded. I was not fainthearted, and shipshape was my love language.

7

My Old Nemesis

Afterward when Hattie and I were standing in front of Frank's building trying to figure out if we should keep walking up the huge hill to the library to get one more reference for my essay from the town historical record, or if we should instead get an ice cream at Stan's Burgers, Hattie said, "I don't think you guys are going to win."

I looked at her. "What're you talking about?"

She shrugged. "You heard what he said."

"So."

"It just seems hard."

"Not for me and Dad."

"But what about all the shipshape stuff?" Hattie said.

"I'm not worried," I said, wiping the sweat off my forehead.

Just then Diego and Leroy rode up on their bikes. They were wearing swimming suits and sunglasses and Diego had a baseball hat on that said *DONE DEAL*.

"Hey, friends," he said.

"Hey," Hattie said. I didn't say hey because I am not his friend. Not when we're both trying to go after the same prize.

"You ready for the big competition?" he asked.

"Yes," I said, narrowing my eyes, which I can do very well. I've practiced.

"Have you turned in your essay?" Diego asked.

The essay was due in one day. Less than twenty-four hours.

"Not yet," I said.

"I turned mine in last Saturday," Diego said.

My jaw dropped! I couldn't help it. Why would he do it that early?

It was fine, I told myself. There were no advantages to getting his essay in early. I had more time to check mine for mistakes. To make it perfect. It was fine.

"My brother, Dan, who's training to be in the UFC, is coming in from Massachusetts tomorrow to be my partner," Diego said.

"His trip is already planned? What if you don't get into the competition?"

He shrugged. "I will."

I swallowed hard. How was he so sure about everything?

"His brother is tough," Leroy said. Leroy and Diego are pretty much inseparable.

"What's UFC?" Hattie asked, and I was glad she did because I had no idea. Universal Fencing Competition? Upset Feline Committee? Underwear Fashion Coalition?

"Ultimate Fighting Championship. It's MMA."

Hattie looked at me. Then she said, "What's MMA?" I do love my sister.

"Mixed martial arts," Diego said. "He's really fast and smart."

How would we compete with an ultimate martial artist? I could handle Diego, but this took it to the next level. I took a deep breath and tried to act natural.

"Well, I don't think there's going to be karate or anything in the competition," I said.

He shrugged. "My brother does karate, but he also does Brazilian jujitsu and Muay Thai, and he was state champion in wrestling when he was in high school. Plus MMA is like ninety percent mental."

I didn't know what Brazilian jujitsu and Muay Thai were, but I did know about wrestling because sometimes we watch it on TV.

"How do you know it's ninety percent mental? No one can prove that," I said.

"Well, I can't *prove* it, but that's what they say."

"That's what who says?"

"The national experts on MMA fighting."

"Oh really? What are the experts' names?"

We all looked at Diego, even Leroy, and he said, "The point is, my brother is a competitor. As in he can compete, C-O-M-P-E-T-E." Diego liked to talk big, but this time it was working.

"Who is *your* partner?" Leroy asked.

"My dad," I said, folding my arms and trying to look big. "Winner of the strawberry eating contest, if you'll remember, against Billy Hogwater."

"Oh," Diego said. He looked scared! He really did! He knew my dad was a tough competitor. He was at the strawberry eating competition. He saw my dad's face, the juice covering his chin and shirt, the determination in his eyes. "He's pretty good."

"He's more than good. He's the best. He has like four books published and he knows everything about Jewel and he ran a marathon once." I thought maybe it was a marathon, but it could have been a 10K. It was back in college, but I didn't tell Diego that. "He's very passionate about Jewel too. He knows everything."

Diego looked nervously at Leroy and I felt euphoric! That's a really good word to describe it. I just looked it up. EUPHORIC!

Diego's brother Dan had nothing on my dad, even if

he was a UFC fighter or whatever. I forgot to write that my dad wore the strawberry mascot costume once in the strawberry parade because the mayor asked him at the last minute because the regular strawberry had the flu. Dad did it, no questions asked, and he even did a few cartwheels. He was a hit!

The more I talked to Diego, the better I felt about the whole thing. Who cared about Dawn Allerton?

"Well, I guess we'll have to see what happens."

"I guess so," I said, pulling my T-shirt away from my skin.

"Do you guys want to go swimming? I have free passes from my dad's work," Diego asked.

"Yes!" Hattie squealed. A huge semi passed, blowing hot air on us.

"We can't," I said, even though jumping in a cool blue pool right then would have felt so good and maybe would have cleared my head. Sometimes when I get overheated I have a hard time thinking and I still needed to find the perfect ending for my essay.

"Why not?" Hattie pouted, bouncing on her toes. It was over ninety degrees outside according to the bank sign.

"We don't have our swimsuits," I replied quickly.

Hattie deflated like a balloon.

"Go get them and meet us at the rec center," Diego said. I swallowed hard. Diego didn't know where we lived.

He didn't know that getting our swimsuits would take us about fifteen hours.

"Actually, I think they're in the wash, but thanks for inviting us."

"Just come," Leroy said. "They put in a new slide this year."

"We can't today, but thanks."

"You're missing out," Diego said.

"Okay, thanks," I said. These guys were relentless.

Finally the two of them rode off. "See you at Strawberry Days!" he yelled.

"See you!" I yelled back.

And then they were gone.

It was just me and Hattie and the blazing hot sidewalk.

"I wish we could've gone," Hattie said.

I nodded. "I know. Just wait. In one week, we'll be swimming every day."

8

The Wait

I turned in my essay at 8:55 Saturday morning, five minutes before it was due.

I thought about Dawn Allerton sitting at her desk reading it. Would she like the introduction? Would she understand my reference to Georgia O'Keeffe? Did I lean too heavy on Strawberry Day folklore?

Dad kept saying, "You okay, Meg?"

And I kept saying, "I'm fine, thank you berry much." I think it's good to stay focused.

I walked to the lake and back four times. This had nothing to do with getting more fit for the competition, though, and everything to do with me getting more and more nervous. I walked until my head hurt and I needed to drink some water. Then me and Hattie dug a hole in the backyard for her My Little Ponies to have a belowground stable. I did five laps around the house on my stilts. I went to bed early because I was tired from the walking and the digging and the stilting and I wanted to get the night over with and get closer to finding out if I was in the competition or not.

I had to be.

I dreamed of strawberries and Diego and Dawn Allerton all night long.

The next day was Sunday.

I walked to the lake and back six times.

I tried to read *Anne of Green Gables* again but kept getting distracted.

I burned a cheese sandwich in the microwave.

I walked around the house ten times on my stilts.

I threw a tennis ball we found in the woods at the shed.

I made Hattie cry because I can't remember why and then I said sorry and she said sorry.

I ate dinner.

Then I went to sleep.

At 11:06 on Monday morning I got an email!

Dear Megan Amelia Stokes,

We are pleased to inform you that you have qualified to participate in the Strawberry Ambassador Competition! The field was large;

however, the judges were impressed with your essay—particularly your discussion of the history of Strawberry Days and the Strawberry Debacle of 1978. Many citizens don't know about that episode in our town's history.

We look forward to being further enlightened by your energy throughout the course of the competition. Please remember that the goal of the Strawberry Ambassador Competition is to find a representative who shares the values our town has been known for throughout the region: hard work, resilience, and charity. We trust you will take this opportunity seriously.

Our opening event will be at the annual Strawberry Pancake Breakfast and Hot-Air Balloon Launch, sponsored by Soelberg Grocery, on Wednesday, June 11, at 7:30 a.m. You and your partner will be introduced by our chairperson for the competition, Dawn Allerton. She will read an excerpt from your essay. You will then have three minutes to let the good citizens of Jewel know who you are, what charity you will be competing for, and why you should be the Strawberry Ambassador.

Please prepare and be at Kiwanis Park no later than 7:15 a.m. Wednesday morning. Major fundraising

events will be held Thursday and Friday, with
a finale on Saturday morning. Details will be
forthcoming.

Thank you and good luck,
Keoni Uluave
Assistant Event Coordinator

I screamed!

I screamed and Hattie screamed and I ran around the
house and Mom and Dad weren't home so I called them
both at work. "We got in! We got in!"

"Of course we got in," Dad said.

"Oh, good," Mom said.

And that's how it all went down and everything was
smooth and perfect and shipshape. The end. End of story.
Done.

Or so I thought.

9

Unexpected News

That afternoon, I went into my room and lay on my bed.

Hattie and I share a tiny room. We have bunk beds—hers is a twin on top. Mine is a double on the bottom, which is just about big enough for me and my stuffed animals—I'm a collector. So that afternoon, I lay on my bed with all my animals.

I had taped the words to the town song and all the trivia stuff along with pictures of strawberries and Leaf bikes under Hattie's bunk bed. Kind of like my own dream board.

I couldn't believe it was starting in two days!!!

And I was in!!!

We were going to win, I could feel it in my bones!!!

I closed my eyes and envisioned riding the Leaf bike to Lin's, the sun in the sky, the birds chirping, Trudy Martin giving me an even bigger bag of taffy, which I put in the cargo compartment beside my tote with my swimsuit and towel. Lin would be waiting on her front porch and we'd go straight to the pool and then we'd go swimming all day, only taking breaks to eat taffy, and then I'd ride the bike home just in time for dinner.

Oh, it was going to be amazing. I couldn't wait. I could not.

I basked in the excitement for at least ten minutes when suddenly I heard the screen door bang.

I sat up.

Who was that?

Hattie was in Mom and Dad's room reading. Did she go outside?

"Hattie?" I called.

No answer.

I heard a cough.

"Dad?"

"Hey," he said. His voice was quiet and it was only three in the afternoon.

"Why're you home?" I got up and walked to the front room. Dad was sitting on the couch, his face red, his baseball cap in his hands.

He didn't look right.

"Are you okay?"

He blew out a long breath of air. "Sit down, bug."

I quickly sat on the chair across from him.

He looked at me like someone was sick.

"I have something to tell you."

I nodded. "Okay."

I thought maybe he was the one who was sick.

But it was worse. It was way, way worse.

"Meg. I can't do the competition with you."

I froze like a Popsicle.

Like my organs turned to ice.

"I found out town employees can't compete . . . I didn't know . . . Got in a big argument . . ."

The words were jumbled.

His face was blurry.

Sounds bounced off the walls and ricocheted around the room.

"Do you understand?"

I couldn't talk.

I could barely breathe.

"Meg. I asked Mom, but she can't get off work. I don't know what to say."

"You have to," I whispered.

"Meg. I'm so sorry."

I shook my head.

I couldn't think.

I tried to think.

I tried to organize my thoughts but I felt like throwing up and I'd just eaten fish sticks, not good.

"Meg," Dad said. "It's not the end of the world. Maybe they'll do the competition again next year."

No.

No.

No.

I stood up.

"Megan," Dad said.

I turned and walked to my room. "Meg."

I closed the door.

I locked the door.

I crawled into my bed.

And I cried.

10

A Deadly Arrival

That night I didn't sleep.

I tossed and turned and every now and then I moaned.

"Are you okay?" Hattie whispered.

I said nothing.

"Meg," she said, hanging over the bunk to look at me, so I rolled over and faced the wall.

She went back up to her bed, where she belonged, and I started moaning again.

What do I do?

What?

I was not giving up. I would never give up.

If Dad couldn't do it, who could? Who could be my partner on such short notice?

Emily Arnold, my PE coach, maybe would, but she went to New York for the summer.

Tessa Nelson, my art teacher? She was nice and painted well but was she driven?

Maybe I could get our mailman to do it? We didn't talk a lot, but he walked briskly.

It was useless. None of them would work.

There was no time.

There was no one.

I couldn't believe it.

The next morning, Tuesday, I slept until 11:48 a.m., which is the latest I have ever slept in my life.

I woke up feeling like soggy bread.

I wanted it to be a bad dream but I knew it wasn't.

I lay in my bed and stared at my stupid strawberry Leaf bike dream board.

I really couldn't believe it.

It had ended before it started.

Dad was in the kitchen.

He turned when I walked in. "Meg, I'm sorry."

I said nothing.

Dad had made pancakes and eggs and bacon. It was his day off from his town job, though he should've been writing.

I sat down and Hattie came in. She was wearing a yellow sundress and how could she? How could she wear yellow on a day like this? How could any of them even walk around and eat pancakes and bacon?

I opted for cold cereal instead.

"Did you get much sleep?" Dad asked, putting a glass of orange juice by me, which I would not drink. I would not.

I shook my head no.

"I told you," Hattie said to Dad.

Dad sighed. "Meg. There's nothing we can do. I'm sorry. I know this feels like a big deal but with time, you'll get over it."

I would not. I would never.

I ate a spoonful of cereal, the milk dripping down my chin like my hopes and dreams. I thought about leaving it there as a reminder of the personal tragedy I was enduring, but it was pretty gross so I wiped it off with a napkin.

I looked at him. "Call the mayor or the council. They know you're an upstanding citizen."

He shook his head. "They can't make any exceptions. We argued for over an hour."

My eyes filled with tears again. I thought I'd cried all the water out of my body. But clearly I hadn't. Maybe I'd cry for the rest of my life.

I stuffed another spoonful of cereal into my mouth, my heart breaking.

And then . . . a sound.

I'll always remember the exact moment we heard it, the sound of the earth rumbling.

I was in my nightgown; I was in the depths of despair and I was chewing soggy cereal.

"What is that?" Hattie said.

We stood up and went to the window. "Oh my gosh," Hattie said.

It was barreling toward us.

"Do you know that truck?" I asked, wiping my eyes.

Dad shook his head. "I have no idea."

It was huge. A huge beat-down green truck. The driver, the silhouette of the driver, looked like a gigantic triangle head. And all of it was heading toward us like an out-of-control train.

It was frightening, I'm not going to lie. Like something out of a horror movie.

"They better slow down or they're going to run right into the house," Dad said.

"Maybe they're lost," Hattie said.

"People who are lost don't drive like that," Dad said.

The truck got closer and closer.

I ran to the front door. Hattie ran after me and Dad wasn't far behind.

The three of us stood on the porch and watched as the truck pulled into the driveway, rammed into the mailbox, and sent our cat Daisy running for the trees.

Hattie grabbed my hand. I grabbed Dad's hand. What was happening?

When the dirt settled, it looked like . . .

No.

No?

Could it be?

The person in the truck was waving furiously at us. She opened the big old door, which made a loud creaking sound like it might fall off its hinges, and Dad said, "Mom?"

Hattie screamed.

She screamed and yelled "GRAM!" and ran to the truck door.

It was my Grandma Sally.

My Grandma Sally, who had gotten some kind of weird hairstyle that looked like a triangle.

My Grandma Sally, who was wearing a patchwork red, orange, and yellow floral jumpsuit. It looked like a clown outfit.

My Grandma Sally, who had just pulled up in a monster truck that most definitely was not her tan compact car.

She had to drop like five feet to get to the ground and almost squashed Hattie.

It was her.

It was really her.

Without Grandpa Arthur.

"What's going on, Dad?" I asked.

He looked at me. "I have no idea."

Grandma hugged Hattie and then hugged my dad, who was mumbling something, and then she came up on the steps to me.

"Grandma," I said. "You're here."

"Hey, sugar bum. Of course I'm here. You ready to take this competition to the next level?"

I stared at her. "What?"

"I just got off the phone with that Dawn Allerton lady your father told me about and I gave her a piece of my mind. I told her how ridiculous it was that your father can't compete and how I was coming all this way to take his place and that she should be ashamed of herself."

"You *what*?" No no no no no no.

"You heard me. I told her she better watch out, the Stokes ladies are about to take the Raspberry Days by storm." She pulled out a matching clown jumpsuit from her bag and handed it to me. "Now, wear this so we can brainstorm properly."

And that was when I fainted.

11

Please Help Me

I know fainting seems extreme. I didn't mean to faint. I just, you know, fell down.

"Oh my goodness," Grandma said.

Dad knelt down next to me and I lay there like a rag doll. I don't know why. It was almost like I needed a few rag doll seconds to get my thoughts together.

"Meg?" Dad said.

"Give me a minute," I whispered.

"What?" he said.

I opened my eyes. "Sorry," I said. "Sorry. I think I just locked my knees or something."

"Oh yes. Don't ever lock your knees. I've fainted twice in rehearsal doing that and it's very dangerous, especially in stilts," Grandma said.

"Get your sister some water," Dad said to Hattie, who ran inside.

I looked up at Grandma from the dirt. "Did you really talk to Dawn Allerton?"

"You better believe I did," Grandma said, squatting down and putting her hand on my forehead.

It was over.

It was all over.

Even if having Grandma as a partner was a good idea, which it was not, getting on the wrong side of Dawn Allerton from the beginning was the mark of death. There was no way we could win. No way.

I sat up. "I'm so sorry you came all this way, Grandma, but I'm not doing the competition with you."

Grandma Sally looked at Dad. "Did the rules change? Did the Dawn woman change her mind?"

"No, she didn't," Dad said.

"Well, who else can do it? Steph has work, right?"

Dad nodded. "Yeah. She does."

I blanched.

"And it starts tomorrow, right?"

Hattie brought the water and I stood shakily, Dad holding my arm, and drank the whole thing in one long gulp. I didn't want to hurt Grandma's feelings but I was not going into a major competition with her. Not wearing matching floral clown jumpsuits. And especially not with Dawn Allerton already poisoned.

"I have some options, Grandma. But thank you. Dad actually might talk to the mayor and still be able to compete."

Dad shook his head. "I can't," he said.

Grandma looked at him. Then she looked at me. Then she looked at Hattie. "Come help me with the suitcases, Hattie Pattie. Time's wasting."

They started pulling suitcases out of the king cab of the truck. It looked like she was moving in for a month. This was weird because usually she and Grandpa stayed at the motel outside town when they came because they liked the pool and we didn't have much space.

"I thought you were going to be Miss Hannigan, Mom," Dad said.

"That's why I called yesterday, Peter. I didn't get the part."

She and Hattie were carrying bags to the front porch.

"You didn't get it?"

Grandma set down a suitcase and said, "No, I did not. They gave it to Ellory Rose, who sang off key and yelled her lines. She *yelled* them. Raquel and I had to plug our ears. We really did. But you know, I'm fine with not getting the part because I can be here." She was talking loud and fast and it didn't seem like she was fine, I'll tell you that.

"What about Dad?" Dad said. "Where's he?"

"He has a work project but he wants full updates." Then she said, "When you said Meggy was in hot water,

I thought, you know what, if the people at Town Center Theater don't need me, I know someone who does. Someone right there." She pointed at me.

I hate it when people call me Meggy. I also hated where this was going.

"Mom. I'm sorry you didn't get the part."

Grandma ignored Dad. Instead she got a basketball out of a garbage sack she'd just pulled out of the truck and threw it to Hattie. "Do you have one of those?"

"No," Hattie said. "We don't have a hoop or anything."

Grandma shrugged. "Neither did we, but where there's a will there's a way." Hattie smiled like she knew what Grandma meant.

"Is this a new outfit?" Dad asked, nodding to her suit.

Grandma was beaming. "Oh, yes! My friend Jackie from my adventuring group has gotten me into upcycling. I made this out of my old housedresses. I made that one for Meg." She pointed at the clown jumpsuit that was now sitting on the front porch, like a bad omen. At least she hadn't insisted I put it on to brainstorm again. "And I've got something I'm working on for all of you. I brought my sewing machine so I can finish them."

"Great," Dad said, although he sounded confused.

"Upcycling?" Hattie asked.

"Yup. It means making your old things into new things. Look at this," she said, showing us a backpack that looked like it was made from old cut-up tennis shoes. "Do either of you want it?"

"I do," Hattie said immediately. I was kind of jealous Hattie spoke up so fast because though I wouldn't dare be seen in public with it, it did look weatherproof.

"And Mom," Dad said, glancing back. "Where did you get that truck?"

She put her hands on her hips, and looked at the truck. "It's pretty, isn't it?"

The bumper looked like it was about to fall off and the paint was chipped on the side. There were some cool stripes, though.

"Sure, but is it yours?" Dad asked.

"I traded my car for it with a kid down the street. He was having a hard time."

"You traded your car for that?" I said.

Grandma Sally shrugged. "Yep."

"With who?"

"One of our neighbor's boys. He just, you know, he was fixing it up to get into those truck shows they do but then he needed something more reliable to take to college so we traded."

I didn't think Mom, Dad, or even Grandpa Arthur would trade in their car for a monster truck. Maybe Hattie would, but it would have to be an accident. This was just Grandma Sally and her new way of life.

"It's biodiesel, by the way, that's why it smells like popcorn and cow farts, so not so bad for the environment, Peter. I know what you're thinking."

It kind of did smell like popcorn and cow farts, or at least horse farts. I'm not as familiar with cows.

"You do not know what I'm thinking, Mom. You do not," Dad said.

She laughed. "That's probably true."

"Is it street legal?" Dad asked.

"What?"

"Street legal."

She looked at the truck. "I think so. Is that a thing with these trucks?"

With Grandma already potentially doing things illegally, we'd never win this competition as partners.

"Dad," I said, and he gave me an exasperated look.

She kept talking. "Anyway, Grandpa Arthur thought it was a strange trade too, but I just told him first of all, we should help the boy out and second of all, I've been wanting a truck for a long time."

"For what?" Dad asked. "Your old car seemed like a much better fit for you, Mom."

"Oh my gosh, Peter. How would I be able to get all this in that tiny car?" She pointed to our porch, which was now crowded with suitcases and garbage sacks. Then she walked to the back of the truck and pulled off a tarp.

"Come help me. All of you," she said.

We walked over and climbed up on the back to see. It was full of boxes. Boxes and sacks and shoes.

"What is all this?" I asked.

"Costumes."

We looked at her. "Why?" Hattie asked.

"For the competition," she said, a sparkle in her eye.

12

Two Histories

Now, there are two accounts of how my grandma ended up in my driveway a day before the competition as related by my dad and Grandma in our front yard. I was still in my pajamas, FYI. And maybe still had some milk on my face, double FYI. And Grandma still had triangle hair, a clown costume on, and a monster truck in our driveway. Triple FYI.

DAD'S STORY:

Grandma called Dad while he was walking home from work to break me the news that he couldn't participate in the competition.

Dad told Grandma the whole strawberry saga.

When he was done, Grandma said, "Well, that's not fair."

And Dad said, "I mean, I do work for the town."

And Grandma said, "It's still not fair. She got in with her essay, she worked for that. She wrote and researched and poured her heart into it and she doesn't get to compete?" (Here, I had to agree with Grandma Sally.)

"Uh, yeah. She can't without a partner, Mom."

"This is ridiculous," Grandma said. "Ridiculous. Nothing is fair in life and I'm sick of it." Dad thought that was a strong reaction, but he appreciated it. He didn't know Grandma had just been rejected as Miss Hannigan.

Dad told her what he didn't want to tell me. "It's going to break Meg's heart."

"She can handle it," Grandma said. "She's got our genes. She's tough. Just rip the Band-Aid off."

He came home, he ripped the Band-Aid off and told me his news, and I started bawling. He had no idea Grandma was coming.

That was Dad's story.

GRANDMA'S STORY

Grandma called Dad to tell him she didn't get the part in *Annie*.

Grandma didn't tell Dad about not getting the part because he told her the strawberry story first, which she thought was ridiculous and she couldn't believe that on top of not getting the part of Miss Hannigan, her granddaughter was being treated like this. "Nothing is fair in life and I'm sick of it," she said.

Once Grandma was off the phone she said to Grandpa, "Arthur, I'm leaving for Jewel tomorrow morning to do a competition with Meg."

Grandpa said, "What're you talking about?"

Grandma said, "I don't have time to tell you everything unless you want to come with me to Susan's house." Susan is my grandma's friend and is in her adventure group, along with Upcycling Jumpsuit Jackie. She is also the costume mistress for the theater across town (not Town Center Theater, which had just insulted my grandmother in the worst way by giving Miss Hannigan to Ellory Rose).

Grandpa went with her to Susan's house in her new old monster truck that may or may not be street legal and Grandma told him all about the competition and how I was raising money for the Alzheimer's Association which was the best thing ever and now I couldn't do it because Dad was a town employee and it was a complete miscarriage of justice and she would not stand for it.

Grandpa thought the whole thing was a bad deal. "But you can't just drive out there. Especially without clearing it with Peter," Grandpa said. He also said, "And I have to work so you'll be alone."

Grandma Sally said, "You bet your buttons I can drive out there without telling Peter. I'm allowed to surprise my granddaughter! And plus, I was planning on going alone."

Grandpa said, "Do you think that's safe, Sally?"

Grandma said, "OH PUFFO." This is one of my Grandma Sally's favorite phrases for when she thinks you're telling her, *You can't do that*.

Grandma also said, "Go bold or go old, Arthur. Go bold or go old." Another favorite phrase, as you'll remember.

Grandpa sighed. Grandma didn't say he sighed. I'm just taking creative license here and I know he sighed. He sighs a lot. Maybe it's an accountant thing.

They went to Susan's house.

Susan had recently told Grandma Sally that she was going to donate a bunch of old costumes and props that they weren't going to use anymore.

When Grandma arrived, she said, "Susan, it's an emergency. I need some of those costumes and props for a very important role."

Susan took her to the warehouse to let her pick out any that were in the discard area, which was a lot.

I said, "I don't understand why we need costumes."

Grandma Sally said, "Shush. Let me finish my story."

There were so many costumes. Her favorites were ones from *The Phantom of the Opera, The Little Mermaid,* and *The Tempest,* which is a really weird Shakespeare play, according to my dad.

Grandma couldn't decide, so Susan said, "Take them all."

Grandma Sally hesitated, but Susan said, "Donate what you don't use." So then Grandma was excited and took everything, and a ton of props including a fake doorway, a large plastic skunk, and a box of old stage makeup.

Grandpa said, "There is no way you can fit all that in my car."

Grandma said, "I'll take the truck."

Grandpa said, "Are you serious? On the freeway?"

Grandma said, "Dead serious."

Grandpa knows when Grandma sets her mind on something, there's no changing it.

He helped her get packed. They also were able to get in some boxes of my dad's baseball cards, a pile of trophies, some old board games, and a bag of my Aunt Jenny's old dolls that were very disturbing.

She left at three a.m. the next day, drank two Diet Cokes, stopped once for gas, and now here she was.

That was Grandma's story.

Dad stared at all the boxes of his stuff and said, "Mom. I don't need all this. Where am I going to put it?"

I couldn't believe it. Like *that* was the biggest issue that needed addressing? Not Grandma speeding to our house with mermaid costumes flying out the bed of her truck planning on usurping the competition?

"We've been enjoying them for all these years, honey, we wanted you to have a chance to cherish them. I'm sure you'll find space," Grandma said.

"Can't you leave them in my bedroom? Or up in Dad's new office?" That was the attic where my dad had to live when he was a kid during the war with Great-Grandpa Jack.

"Your dad still uses his office, we're renting Grandpa Jack's apartment in the basement, and I'm turning your bedroom into a vocal studio," Grandma explained.

"Excuse me?" Dad said, and I am going to stop telling about this conversation because it got a little dicey. I guess Dad didn't want his room to change and now I think he knew just a teeny, tiny little bit how it felt to change partners on me unexpectedly.

When everything was finally sorted out, I once again asked the question that had been burning in my heart and soul. "Why do we need all these costumes, Grandma?"

She smiled! A very wicked smile! "Why you ask?"

She reached over and pulled a green spiky wig out of a bag and put it on my head. Just plopped it down like it was a beanie or something.

"We need them because, though we don't know what the challenges are for this competition, we do know how to put on a show. We are going to be the most fabulous contestants for Raspberry Ambassador this town has ever seen. I promise you that."

"Strawberry, Grandma. Strawberry."

"Oh yes. Strawberry. What difference does it make?"

I was doomed.

13

Oh Puffo

For the record, I don't know how to put on a show.

I have never known how to put on a show.

I know how to study for a test. I know how to win the fifth-grade Risk tournament. I know how to beat Diego in the science fair. And I knew we could win the competition without putting on a show.

Dad didn't seem too happy either, probably because he had to go through his stuff and who knew what Mom was going to say about all his old baseball cards or the weird dolls, so I decided to go straight to the source and set up some ground rules for this partnership before it could wreak more flattened mailboxes or worse.

"I don't put on shows, Grandma," I said. "I'm not wearing costumes."

"Oh puffo, of course you are." She was getting a few more things out of the truck and I was following her around.

"No. I'm not."

"You are," she said. "But let's work that out later. Can I put my suitcase in your room?"

"What?"

"I want to get settled."

I stared at her, confused.

"I'll help you," Hattie said.

Our house only had two bedrooms, Dad's writing loft that had more spiders than windows, the kitchen, the bathroom, and the front room that had a sloped ceiling because of the porch. There was no space for houseguests. Again, that was why my grandparents always got a motel room when they visited.

"Are you staying with us?" I asked, trailing after Hattie and Grandma into our room.

"Of course, I need to be close to the action." She plopped her purse on the floor.

"But where are you going to sleep?"

"Right here," she said, sitting ON MY BED!

I stood in the doorway. "There?"

"Sure. With you. We need to strategize and plan whenever an idea strikes us. We would be at an extreme disadvantage if I was clear across town."

There was no room for Grandma on my bed. None. I mean I guess technically there sort of was room. SORT OF. But not really. Not really and especially not enough room for her ideas that strike her in the middle of the night.

She lay back on the mattress, right in the middle of all my stuffed animals. My octopus got shoved off. Hattie lay down beside her. I didn't move.

"Come," Grandma Sally said, patting the other side of her where my octopus had once been.

I was going to be sleeping with Grandma in my bed.

Grandma was going to be my partner.

Grandma thought I was going to put on a show.

Grandma yelled at Dawn Allerton.

"Come on, goose. Don't be silly. Cuddle up to your grandma."

I sighed and lay down next to her. This was a lot to take in and I wasn't sure how it was going to work out with us winning.

She pulled me close and she smelled like coconut and flowers and she was soft and warm. Even though I had no idea what was going to happen next, and I was scared—very, very scared—it felt good to be next to her.

"I've missed you both so much," Grandma said, holding each of our hands.

"We missed you too, Grandma," I said.

She saw the strawberry pictures and the town song lyrics

and the Jewel facts. "It's a dream board! You're really serious about this competition, aren't you, Meg?"

"I'm so serious, Grandma."

"She really is," Hattie said.

Grandma smiled. "I love to see passion. I do." She turned to me. "Look at my face."

I looked at her.

"Look at my face," she said again.

"I am looking at your face."

"No. *Really* look at my face."

I tried to *really* look at her face. "You see these lines? These wrinkles? This age spot?"

She let go of our hands and she pointed to a brown circle on her cheek.

"Yes."

"These all equal wisdom. They equal experience. They equal spirit." She took a deep breath and closed her eyes and said, "Do you trust me?"

I hesitated. Grandma Sally had always been great. I loved her. But could I trust her in the most important competition of my life? Shouldn't she be trusting me?

"Meg, do you trust me? I can only do this if you trust me." She reached out, her eyes still closed, and patted my face.

I looked at Hattie, who was watching this whole thing like it was a movie.

I didn't have any other options. I really didn't when her hand was holding on to my nose.

"I trust you, Grandma," I said, my voice cracking.

Her eyes flew open. "Do you really?"

"Yes," I said, more resolutely.

"I believe you. I think we can win this thing."

"Okay," I said, and she smiled and hugged me again.

"Now let's get to work," she said.

14

Unforgettable

"This is perfect. This is absolutely perfect," Grandma said to herself after I caught her up on the details for the Strawberry Pancake Breakfast and our speech. Her face was very close to the computer screen that the acceptance email was on even though she was wearing gigantic orange glasses. "Three minutes to make a huge splash and then get out, that's the ticket. You always want to leave them wanting more."

It was getting close to dinnertime and I felt like Grandma had been here ten years. "I mean, is it a splash that we need? Or a well-crafted speech?" I asked.

"Oh, Meg, lead with your heart, my girl. Speeches are boring," Grandma said.

That was rude. How did she know my speech wouldn't

be heart-led? And boring? Who said speeches had to be boring?

She stood up from the computer and said, "Follow me, girls," and marched into our bedroom.

Grandma was trying to take charge. I was coming around to the fact that she was my only hope for the competition, but I was *not* going to give her control.

Nevertheless, I followed her.

"Hattie, can you bring us that box in the front room with the green marker on it?" Grandma asked.

Hattie left and I really didn't think she'd be back any time soon because there were so many boxes, but she was fast, pushing this big box ahead of her. *MISC* was written in bold lettering on top.

Grandma opened it and rummaged through all kinds of things. Bandanas, mustaches, a fake rabbit. My stomach started to feel queasy. She yanked out a big, black thing. "There we go," she said.

She held it up. It was a tuxedo jacket with tails and sequins on it.

"Hold on to this," she said, and put it on my lap.

She rummaged some more and pulled out another one.

"Grandma, what are you doing?" I said.

"Now hang on. Bear with me."

Out came a top hat.

And another top hat.

White shirts.

Black sequin pants.

Red bow ties and belt things all followed until my eyes were swimming.

"This is what we're wearing tomorrow morning for the pancake breakfast," she said.

Now my stomach was full-on hurting.

"I absolutely am not wearing that," I said. No one would take me seriously if my entire outfit reflected back at them, not to mention I'd never seen let alone owned as many sequins in my entire life.

She put on one of the top hats. "This is what the Phantom wore in *The Phantom of the Opera* in our city production. It's iconic."

"But why are there two costumes if there's only one Phantom?" Hattie asked.

"One for the Phantom, and one for the understudy." She winked at me. Oh my gosh. Was I the understudy? Me?

"Grandma," I said, working to stay calm, "I'm not wearing this."

"We'll see." She put the other top hat on my head, stood up, and started taking off her weird jumpsuit.

I turned and looked at the wall. "Grandma, I'm not kidding."

"You just said you trusted me."

"I know, but the competition isn't a play. It's about the

town and strawberries and about, you know, our heritage. It's serious." It felt cheesy to say it like that but it was really how I felt.

She ignored me! She just kept putting on the clothes. I wasn't looking, but it seemed like that was what she was doing given all the rustling. "Hurry up, Meg. Get dressed and let's get working on our speech," she urged.

Hattie was smiling at me and I started to panic.

"Put it on," Hattie said.

I glared at her.

I didn't want to do this. It had all spun out of control so fast, so quickly. "Grandma," I said, glancing at her. "Let's slow down and talk about this." I thought maybe she'd listen to reason, maybe, but she didn't even stop tying her shoes. It was no use.

"Go ahead, goose," Grandma said. "We don't have much time."

I grabbed the stupid pants and jacket and belt thing that I found out was called a cummerbund and went to the bathroom and changed.

You should have seen it.

Really and truly.

It was the worst.

Even worse than the maroon velvet dresses Mrs. Owens

made us wear for the choir concert last year, and those things were tight and scratchy. At least there were fifty other girls wearing them. Not this time. This time it was me and my grandma. Nowhere to hide.

"What's going on in there?" Grandma asked, knocking on the door like a drum.

"It's huge," I said.

"Let me see."

"No, thank you," I said.

"Open the door," Grandma said.

"No."

"Open it, Meg."

I couldn't believe this was happening to me. I opened the door.

There was Grandma in her full tuxedo and it looked like it was made for her. She actually looked good. Like a triangle-haired lady *Phantom of the Opera*.

Then there was me. Me in saggy pants that were falling down and a huge white shirt, a ridiculous bow tie, and a jacket with puffy shoulder pads.

Hattie couldn't stop laughing.

"Stop that, Hattie," Grandma said, but she was smiling. "We just need to, hmm, turn around."

I turned around, heat rising to my face like an oven.

"Give me your ponytail holder, Hattie."

Soon Grandma had bunched up the back of my jacket

and I guess secured it with the ponytail holder so it sort of fit. Sort of. She tied the shirt in the back too and she rolled the top of the pants.

"Grandma, this is crazy."

"No, it's not. We can fix it."

"We can't fix it."

"Oh, we can. We have all afternoon and I told you I brought my sewing machine."

Then she put the top hat back on me and pulled me to the mirror in Mom and Dad's room.

It was bad. It was *so* bad.

Hattie covered her mouth.

"I love it!" Grandma said. "This is perfect."

We heard the back door open and Dad's voice. "Mom. I really don't have room for the baseball . . ." He showed up in the doorway, his voice trailing off.

"Wow," he said, smirking. Was he smirking?

"Isn't it perfect for the opening ceremonies presentation?" Grandma said.

"It's a strawberry pancake breakfast, Grandma. We don't have to dress up."

"Oh puffo. What do you think, Peter?"

I could always count on Dad. Always.

"Uh," he said. "Well . . ." He had to come through. He had to. "You know, one thing's for sure," he said. "No one will forget you."

I gaped.

My dad, Peter Stokes, who wrote in his book *The War with Grandpa* these exact words, check for yourself: *When I grow up and have a kid I will never make him do anything he really does not want to do.*

Dad wrote that!

And he wrote, *This is a solemn promise, so help me God.*

He did say there were some exceptions, like we had to brush our teeth and not play with matches or poison and he'd make us go to school. But tuxedos were not an exception!

"Dad," I said in desperation. "Remember your promise?"

"What promise?"

They were all staring at me. "The promise in your book that you wouldn't make your kids do anything they didn't want to?"

Dad smiled. "Oh, *that* promise."

"Yes, *that* promise."

He shrugged. "Meg, you want to win this competition, right? I think Grandma is on to something here."

My dad, my *ally,* was now a traitor.

15

Early-Morning Drills

The next morning Grandma got up at five.

I did not.

It was still dark outside, the sun was barely coming up, and Grandma whispered to me, "It's time, Meg."

I lay there like a rock. I would not be moved.

She tried again. "Meg. Come on," she whispered. "We have to get ready."

I swallowed hard. All night long I'd tossed and turned, worrying about what I was going to do about the costume. Meanwhile, right next to me, Grandma happily slept the hours away, and now she was up at the crack of dawn.

Grandma put her hand on my cheek. "Wake up, goose. Let's get going."

I opened one eye, trying to be very brave. "Go ahead," I whispered. "I've decided not to wear the tuxedo."

She knelt next to me. "What?"

"I'm not doing it."

"Meg, sweetie, you're doing it."

"No," I whispered, my voice betraying me.

She was quiet. Then she said, "Meet me in the kitchen when you're done getting dressed." And then she left! Just like that.

I lay there.

And lay there.

And lay there.

Finally, I'm ashamed to admit, finally I did get up. I got up. I put on sequin pants. I put on a white shirt. I put on a sequin cummerbund or whatever. I put on a sequin jacket.

Why, you may ask, why would I give in?

Now remember, dear reader, this was before the official war was declared. At that point, I thought Grandma was harmless and had decided to help me win because my dad couldn't be my partner. I didn't want to hurt her feelings. She'd just lost the part of Miss Hannigan. She was fragile, after all.

But no.

Oh no.

Oh no no no no no no.

I found out very soon that I was wrong.

I was so wrong.

Wrong wrong wrong.

Wronger than slimy carrots in your sack lunch.

The wrongest.

Grandma was not fragile. NOT AT ALL.

And here's the thing: looking back at little baby me, who didn't know what she was up against, I choose to forgive myself for wearing the tuxedo. Sometimes you do what you gotta do to get through the day, and I really, really wanted to win those bikes.

So I put on the tuxedo and I gave myself a pep talk:

We had written a speech.

It was good.

It was really good.

We'd practiced it over and over again.

We gave it to Dad and Hattie.

We gave it to Daisy the cat and to the horses down the road, which Grandma loved. She always took them apples when she came to visit.

We gave it to my mom, who, by the way, had hugged and hugged Grandma when she got home from work. Mom was thrilled Grandma was there. Thrilled!

Did she see the monster truck and fallen mailbox outside? Did she see the boxes of costumes and suitcases? Was she at all worried that Grandma was going to ruin my chances at winning the Leaf bikes? If any of those fears were in my mom's mind, you would've never known it.

"Thank you, Sally," Mom kept saying over and over again. "Thank you so much."

Mom didn't even get mad about all the boxes everywhere, and I was counting on that. She just stepped over them and kept saying, "You dropped everything to come help us, Sally? You're a saint."

"I wouldn't call me a saint," Grandma said.

And Mom said, "Well, I would."

I knew I had to make Mom see the truth.

"She's sleeping in my bed," I said with a knowing look.

Mom looked at me. "Oh. Your bed?"

"Yup," I said.

That's right, Mom. MY BED. I thought for sure Mom would say something then like, *How about the couch?* or *We could put up a tent outside* or even *Wouldn't the motel be more comfortable?*

But no. No. My mom said, "Hey. That's fun. I hadn't thought of that. With Arthur not here, I guess there's plenty of room with the girls. It will be like a big sleepover."

MY WHOLE FAMILY WAS AGAINST ME.

Anyway, the point is, I felt like we had a strong speech and maybe people wouldn't notice my shiny tuxedo if I stood behind Grandma.

After my pep talk that didn't really pep me up, I put the final touch on, the dumb top hat, and stared at myself in the mirror.

Why?

I heard Grandma talking on the phone. Probably to Grandpa Arthur. I couldn't hear the conversation except for when she said she was very excited and he should see me in my outfit. Ugh.

When she was done talking, I went out.

"Oh, you look perfect," Grandma said, whispering and squishing my face between her hands. "Perfect!"

"Thank you," I muttered. I couldn't believe I was doing this.

Then she said, "Now for makeup."

"What? Makeup?"

"Please?" she said. "A little goes a long way and we're going to be up on stage."

"Grandma. I don't wear makeup."

"I know, but it's part of the costume, sis." She patted a stool in the kitchen. "Let's do it in here."

"Grandma," I said. "This is going too far."

"Come on. Don't be a stick in the mud."

This was the first time I'd heard Grandma use that phrase in reference to me and I wasn't a stick in the mud. That was one thing I was not.

I sat on the stool and Grandma put on an apron—a makeup apron?—and started painting my face.

"Wow, Grandma. It's so sticky," I said. She was slathering stuff on with a gigantic sponge.

"That means it's working," she said. "You have to go heavy when you're going under the lights."

"What? We're not going to be under lights. What lights?"

She took a step back to look at her work. "On the stage. Stage lights."

"It's a pancake breakfast. There will be no lights. Also, you said a little goes a long way."

She squinted and rummaged in her box for who knows what. "In general, a little goes a long way and really, you shouldn't be wearing makeup. Not for a long time. But for things like this, performances"—she pointed a purple pencil at me—"up on stage, lights or not, you really have to cake it on."

Sweat started to bead on my forehead. That could not be good.

When she finally finished, she held up a mirror. I almost screamed in terror. "Grandma!" I said.

"Shhh," she said. "You'll wake everyone up." And then she said, "I love it. It's theatrical."

"It's awful. I look like an owl."

"Oh puffo. It's perfect. Don't be so dramatic."

I could've died. I really could have.

16

A Little Help from My Friend

At six forty-five we pulled up to Kiwanis Park in Grandma's truck. Grandma drove, Dad sat in front, and me and Hattie were in the backseat. It was a huge truck. Dad had been very supportive of the caked-on makeup, by the way. He said, "Oh, what's this?" when he saw my face.

And before I could say, *HELP! DAD! MAKE IT STOP!* Grandma swooped in and explained about the stage and the lights and how crucial it all was.

"Wow, Meg," Dad said. "How lucky you are to have your grandma here to help you. I had no idea."

Lucky?

Anyway, Grandma drove to the park and the whole way she sang Dolly Parton with the windows down.

Dad sang too.

That's one thing they both love, belting songs.

Hattie was smiling her face off.

And I was about to explode.

Dogs running in waves. Dogs running in waves. Dogs running in waves.

Kiwanis Park is huge. There's a bunch of soccer fields, two playgrounds, pavilions, a baseball diamond, and a running track. It's where the Strawberry Days stuff happens because they need all the space. On the first day of the festival there is always a strawberry pancake breakfast with tons of picnic tables and millions of pancakes. At the end at least ten hot-air balloons go up. This year was the 100th celebration, though, so I knew it would be even bigger.

Grandma was impressed when we got there. "Wow," she said. "They're serious about this thing, aren't they?"

The balloons were laid out all over the soccer fields and across from that, over by the playground, was a big stage with a sign that said *TOWN OF JEWEL STRAWBERRY DAYS CENTENNIAL CELEBRATION*.

There was also a serving area where people were setting up griddles and syrups and then like a hundred tables and chairs. Dad had a bunch of griddles he had to bring too. Grandma was thrilled when Dad asked if we could drive her truck over. "See?" Grandma said when we were loading up. "Isn't the truck wonderful?"

The best part of the Strawberry Pancake Breakfast this year was that on the stage were two Leaf bikes. As Grandma would say, *Be still, my heart.*

"I told you, Mom," Dad said. "It's pretty exciting. It's the best time of year."

Dad seemed sad. He'd brought water and fruit snacks for us to keep in our pockets for energy. He was wearing his *JEWEL* baseball hat that he got when he played softball on the municipal team and his Shakespeare T-shirt from *The Merry Wives of Windsor* that says *Experience is a jewel, and it need be so, for it is often purchased at an infinite rate.*

I hadn't really thought about his feelings in all this. He looked at me from the front seat and smiled. "You can do this," he said. "You can get those bikes."

"Sure," I said, fighting back tears. He should have tried harder. He should have found a loophole. This was *our* competition.

When Grandma parked the truck, we got out and I almost fell on my face because the ground was about twenty feet from the truck door and I was holding our gigantic Alzheimer's Association poster.

"Careful, Megs," Grandma said. "We don't want to get injured before we start."

"I know, Grandma," I said.

I was not feeling good. I had a pound of makeup on my face. I was wearing a glittery straitjacket. And my grandma was giving me advice about a contest that up until yesterday, she had been calling the Raspberry Competition.

Ugh.

One thing was for sure: I was dying to see who the other people competing would be.

Frank Biddulph was mixing pancake batter. Dad and Hattie carried over the griddles to join him.

"Oh look," Grandma said. "There's a strawberry-shaped balloon."

"Yeah," I said. "A lady named Melanie Bacon pilots that one. It's here every year."

The strawberry balloon had been around since before I was born. Melanie Bacon and her brother used to do the hot-air balloon with their dad when they were kids. Now that her dad was retired and her brother had moved away, she did the balloon all by herself along with her balloon team. She worked at Soelberg Grocery and she liked to tell me about all the adventures she and the strawberry balloon went on.

"I'm going to talk to her," Grandma said.

I shrugged. "It starts in fifteen minutes. Don't be late."

"Sounds good, goose," she said, and walked toward the balloons.

I saw Lin and her dad getting out of their car.

"Lin!" I yelled.

She walked slowly toward me, like she was confused. Was something wrong?

I jogged over.

She froze. "Oh my gosh," she said. "Is that you? Meg?"

"Yes, it's me."

She was in shock. She was in actual shock, like I wondered if I should call a paramedic. "What is happening? I barely recognize you," she said, her hand to her face.

"What are you talking about?"

She circled around me. "I mean, it kind of looks like you, like it's the same general shape, but—" She came around to my front, her face red, like she was going to burst out laughing.

"I could also be a penguin," I said.

Her dad walked up and he was confused too. "Meg?"

I tried to remain calm. Grandma said in the face of uncertainty, remain calm. We'd had a lot of talks in bed last night before she put her CPAP machine on. Benefits of not staying in a motel, she reminded me.

"Hello, Meg?" her dad said again.

"Hello, Larry." That's her dad's name. "How was camping?"

Then Lin started laughing. Like laughing and laughing and laughing. "I'm so sorry," she said. "I'm just. Oh my gosh. I'm so sorry. Why are you wearing that? Are they making you wear that? Does everyone have to wear that? Where's your dad? Is he wearing a costume?"

In all the awfulness and excitement I'd forgotten to call and tell Lin that I'd had a change of partner.

Once she got ahold of herself I told her the news. "My dad isn't competing."

"What?" she gasped.

We walked toward the pancake area. Lin's dad was also a volunteer cook and he and Lin were carrying more griddles. It was griddle heaven.

"I have so much to tell you."

"I want to know everything," she said. Lin really was the best, even if she laughed, but I would have laughed too—I looked like a whole different person.

First we went and touched the bikes.

Oh the bikes, the loves of my life.

They were yellow and the word *LEAF* was painted on them in green. The cargo bags were just as big as they said online. I kind of wanted to hug them and whisper *I'll be seeing you soon,* but I resisted.

We sat at the contestants' table and I told Lin all the gory details. The truck, the jumpsuits, the costumes.

"She brought costumes?"

"So many costumes. Like hundreds of them."

"Hundreds?"

"I don't know. A lot."

"Oh my gosh, I love your grandma. I want to see them all." Lin likes things like costumes. I do not.

Right then, I saw Diego and his brother coming across the field.

I wanted to sink into the ground. "Hide me," I said to Lin.

"That's going to be hard. You're about to get up on the stage in front of the whole town."

"I know, just, oh man. I can't believe this is happening."

"Hey, guys," Diego said. "Uh, Meg?"

I looked at him with confidence because I decided to fake it to make it. That was another piece of my grandma's advice last night, by the way. "How can I help you?"

"Um, why are you dressed like that? Did some tap dancer die?"

"What?"

"You look like you're going to a tap dancer's funeral."

Lin started laughing again. "I'm sorry," she said mid-laugh. I tried to forgive her.

"What are you talking about?" I said, in a loud voice. "This is from the *Phantom of the Opera*."

"From a ghost?"

Lin looked at him. "No, an opera."

Diego shrugged. "A ghost or an opera, I don't care. I just am very glad Meg decided to wear it because it has made my day so much better."

I folded my hands across my chest. "I'm glad I could help out," I said.

Diego laughed. "But for real, what happened to you?"

"Her grandma did it," Lin said.

"Who?"

"My grandma."

"Your grandma?"

I sighed. "Yes. My grandma." Right then, like magic, Grandma Sally appeared.

"You rang?" she said.

And that's how Diego met my partner and found out he was probably going to win the Strawberry Ambassador Competition.

I could write more.

I could write about how Diego's brother looked like the Incredible Hulk. A not-green Incredible Hulk who was going to medical school, and Lin whistled! She whistled!

"I thought you said he was training for the UFG," I said.

"It's actually UFC," his brother said, "and I am doing that and school."

I could write about the chitchat Grandma made with Diego's brother and how he said we looked like Phantoms from the *Phantom of the Opera*. He really did say that and he hadn't heard the earlier conversation.

Grandma about peed her pants, she was so excited. "Did you hear that, Meg? Did you hear that?"

"I did hear that, Grandma."

I could write so many things but for now, I will move forward.

The other kids began to arrive and it wasn't looking good, who we were up against.

First came Ellie Hansen, who goes to the other elementary school and who won the district spelling bee and was a star soccer player and one time sang a solo at the town Trunk or Treat. She showed up with her mom. Ellie was wearing a button-down blue dress and her mom was in a blue skirt and white shirt. They blended in with the pancake griddle crowd.

Cooper Hedengren and Mr. Bailey, our teacher, came next, which was kind of surprising but not too surprising. Cooper lived with his mom and his brother and like fifty dogs. He was nice and he one time gave me a pack of Mentos after school. Mr. Bailey was Cooper's uncle. Both of them were in jeans and T-shirts. What I wanted to wear.

And finally Zoe Jackson arrived. Zoe does homeschool but she comes to our school fairs sometimes. She once won a short story contest that was published in a national magazine and got on the news. She was with her dad and he was in a nice shirt and dress pants and she was wearing a zippered skirt. Business casual. Good choice.

No one else was wearing tuxedos and top hats.

No one else had evil eyebrows and gallons of makeup.

No one else had my grandma for a partner.

I slumped in my seat.

17

The Smell of Fear

A lot of people came to the Strawberry Pancake Breakfast because of the hot-air balloons and because it only cost five dollars for the most delicious pancakes and okay eggs and sausage and orange juice. Companies shut down to take their employees. It was a big deal.

I kept trying to be calm and normal but really I wanted to shrink and disappear into the grass. Later, Dad, trying to make me feel better, said, "You seemed like you were fine sitting up there," and I said, "Dad, at no time, no time, was I fine. Never. If anything I was the opposite of fine."

So we were all sitting there and Dawn Allerton walked up with a clipboard. My throat went dry. There was a man who looked like a mouse following her. He was holding a briefcase and a plate of pancakes. Her assistant? Keoni from my acceptance letter? Dawn was wearing a gray suit. Her hair was pulled back tight and it looked like she meant business.

"Hello. Welcome to the Strawberry Pancake Breakfast. We're excited to have you here and to introduce you to the people of Jewel—your hopeful charitable contributors." She looked down the row of us and stopped when she landed on Grandma and me.

A look of distaste crossed her face. It really did.

Grandma grabbed my hand and I tried to remain strong. The final piece of wisdom Grandma had handed out last night was that some people might disapprove of us for whatever reason. Maybe because they'd been yelled at on the phone? I suggested. Whatever reason, Grandma had said.

"We will embrace the disapproval. We will draw energy from it. We have to stand out from the crowd and sometimes, people who are different get ridiculed," she'd said.

And now here we were.

I tried to embrace the distaste. I tried to draw energy from it.

It was pretty dang hard.

"The town will be donating two hundred fifty dollars to each of your charities for just showing up," Dawn said. She stopped and waited for us to clap. I clapped very loud.

"Now, a few things. First, you're in partnerships. Part

of the competition will be to see how well the two of you work together." Grandma squeezed my hand.

"Second, once we get things started I will announce each partnership to the crowd and then I will read an excerpt from the essays you submitted to get into the competition. Then I will turn the time over to you for your speeches."

That was good. I had put a lot of time and passion into my essay and maybe it would supersede our tuxedos. Is *supersede* the right word?

Dawn went on. "Third, some of you may not have extensive experience on stage."

Grandma raised her hand.

Dawn glanced our way, a look of irritation crossing her face. "What are you doing?" I whispered.

Grandma raised her hand higher.

"Um, yes?" Dawn said.

"I'm actually a student of the stage. If you'd like me to give some tips to my fellow competitors . . ."

"That won't be necessary," Dawn said before Grandma could finish.

Diego looked at me and winked, so I winked right back.

Dawn kept talking. "Please speak directly into the microphone and try to enunciate your words."

Grandma whispered in my ear about projecting sound from my stomach but I wouldn't listen. Instead I sat up and showed Dawn I was being attentive.

"The hot-air balloons will be launched near the end of the speeches. This was not my idea, I'll have you know. In fact I think it will be distracting but the powers that be, I'm not naming names"—she looked over at a couple people standing by the pancake table—"some people thought it would be a good idea."

This was just the beginning of Dawn Allerton's instructions.

As she spoke, Grandma seemed to be taking mental notes. I, on the other hand, sat as crouched as I could because more and more people were showing up. I had never seen so many people at the Strawberry Pancake Breakfast in my life. Were they here because of the Strawberry Ambassador Competition?

Finally, Dawn Allerton announced the order for our speeches. This was VERY important. We needed to go soon. As soon as possible. My face was starting to itch, my heart was thumping, and Grandma kept raising her hand, which was annoying Dawn Allerton to high heaven, as my Grandpa Arthur would say. The sooner we got this over with, the better.

"We'll start with Diego and Dan Martinez," Dawn said. Diego seemed happy with that. "Then we'll have Ellie and Tamara Hansen."

Please, us next. Please, us next.

"Then we'll have Cooper Hedengren and Rich Bailey."

Okay, fine. Just not last. Not last.

"Next will be Zoe and Mark Jackson."

Of course. What else could go wrong?

Dawn Allerton looked at Grandma and me again, and her nose crinkled like we smelled bad. Like we SMELLED bad. How dare she! "Coming in the rear, we'll have the dapper duo here, Meg and Sally Stokes."

"Thank you!" Grandma said cheerfully.

Dawn gave her a look and handed her clipboard to the guy.

Diego looked over at me and mouthed, *Sorry*.

I think he genuinely felt bad for me, and I didn't blame him.

18

My Grandma, the Gazelle

Dawn got up on the stage and spoke into the microphone.

"Good morning, everyone, and welcome to the town of Jewel's 100th Strawberry Days!"

Cheers. Clapping. Yelling.

My stomach started churning.

"We are thrilled to introduce the winners of our essay contest and the contestants in our Strawberry Ambassador Competition."

Grandma whispered, "I am so happy to be a part of this. I am so, so happy."

"Okay, Grandma," I whispered. "Okay."

"We are going to start with Diego and Daniel Martinez, who are from a family who have lived in this town for many years. I'll read an excerpt from Diego's essay and then let them introduce themselves," Dawn said.

She began to read, and Diego's essay was good. He talked about his great-grandparents immigrating to the United States and what home means and love and oh my gosh, Grandma was crying. Should my grandma be crying? Should she be so clearly rooting for our competition? She even blew her nose louder than a foghorn, for all to see and hear.

The crowd went wild when Dawn finished Diego's excerpt and Grandma Sally stood up. "Marvelous!" she said to Diego. "Just marvelous!"

Diego did a bow to Grandma and then to the crowd. Barf. And then he and Dan got up on the stage. Diego waved at me and Grandma said, "He's such a nice boy."

I nodded. "He's okay."

Then Dan got out a guitar.

"Hey, everyone, I'm Dan."

"And I'm Diego and we thought we'd sing our introduction because music is life."

They then proceeded to harmonize an original song about strawberries and Jewel.

At the end, again the crowd going wild, Grandma leaned over. "We need to up our game."

Before I could ask what she meant, Dawn got back up.

Diego sat down by me and said, "I believe in you."

I stuck out my tongue.

Ellie's essay was also good. Then their speech was amazing. Grandma shifted in her chair.

When Cooper and Mr. Bailey got up there, Grandma whispered, "I have an idea."

"What?"

"I have an idea."

"What idea?" Now my stomach was churning so hard that my breakfast was turning into butter. What idea did Grandma have? What was she thinking? *Oh please, Grandma. Please just be normal. Please.* This was why I wanted to go first.

Dawn looked over at us and scowled. I buttoned my lip.

When Cooper and Mr. Bailey were done, Grandma said, "When the next group gets up there, after she reads the essay, bring the Alzheimer's Association sign and follow me."

"Follow you where?"

"Shhh," someone said.

Dawn started reading Zoe's essay and I leaned over to Grandma and said, "We can't leave. We're next."

"Trust me, Meg. Trust me."

Oh my gosh. I looked back at Lin. She gave me a thumbs-up. I looked at Dad. He smiled and mouthed, *You got this.*

I needed someone to help me. Help me keep Grandma from going rogue, otherwise Dawn might disqualify us. We couldn't go anywhere right now. We couldn't have *ideas* at a time like this. We were about to go on stage!

"Stick with the plan, Grandma," I hissed.

"Meg," she said, as Zoe and her dad were walking up the stairs to the stage, "trust me."

Then she got down, wiggled out of her chair, slunk between the tables, and started low-running toward the hot-air balloons, which at this point were all blown up and lifting off into the sky one by one like Dawn said they would.

Diego looked at me. "Did your grandma just run away?"

My head was pounding.

"She's going to the bathroom," I said, but we were both watching her cross the field like a gazelle. She went straight to the strawberry balloon.

Then Melanie said something to her. Grandma said something back. On the stage Zoe was talking and her dad was holding up pictures of wildlife.

I looked back at Grandma and SHE WAS IN THE STRAWBERRY BALLOON BASKET waving her arms at me like she was alone on a desert island and had spotted a plane.

"Whoa," Diego said. "Was this part of your presentation?"

I closed my eyes. What was I going to do? Do I get on the stage alone? Do I hide in the truck? What was she doing??? I looked at those Leaf bikes, those beautiful Leaf bikes.

"Meg," Diego whispered. "Is that even allowed?"

"I don't know," I whispered back.

Zoe's dad was talking now. They were almost done. I

was sweating great drops of brown foundation. I had no choice. She was my partner and we had to stick together. Those were the rules. I looked at Diego. "Wish me luck," I said, then grabbed our charity sign and ran toward the giant strawberry.

19

Our Speech

When I was about halfway across the field, Dawn Allerton got on the PA system and said, "Next we have Meg and Sally Stokes."

Then she got quiet.

I kept running. It was a lot farther than it looked, and the poster was kind of hard to manage.

"Meg Stokes? Sally Stokes?"

I guess someone said something, probably Diego, and she saw me, because suddenly her voice came booming over the microphone, like she was yelling into it. "Will the girl in the top hat in the middle of the field stop immediately."

I froze.

"Meg Stokes, is that you?" Dawn said.

The hot-air balloons were loud from all the fire the pilots were using to keep them blown up. I looked over at the stage. The entire crowd was looking at me. Dad was standing up.

Then I heard a different noise.

Grandma had Melanie Bacon's megaphone, and she said, "Keep coming, Megan Amelia, keep coming!"

"Meg Stokes?" Dawn Allerton said. "Would you like to participate or not?"

What a question! The worst question in the world!

"I would like to participate!" I yelled, but there was no way anyone could hear me.

Instead they probably heard Grandma, who must have been projecting from her stomach into the megaphone because her voice boomed into the air, "Dawn Allerton! Please continue the program! Read the excerpt of Meg's essay and we will be ready for our part."

"What?" Dawn said.

Grandma waved at me to come and then she said, "Meg Stokes, proceed to the strawberry balloon. And Dawn Allerton, the show must go on!"

The tuxedo now seemed like the least worst part of this situation.

"Do not go to the strawberry balloon, Meg Stokes," Dawn said.

I looked over at the stage.

Then back at Grandma.

"Megan." Grandma was waving at me furiously. "Trust me!"

119

And so I did.

I felt like I had to.

She was my partner. Dawn deliberately said, *stick with your partner.* If I went back, alone, it would be all over.

I ran toward Grandma, who gave me a triumphant fist pump.

"Go ahead and read her essay!" Grandma yelled into the megaphone.

There was no way Dawn was going to do it.

It was all over.

I got to the balloon just as Dawn's voice came over the PA.

" 'Why I Love Strawberry Days,' by Meg Stokes."

I turned and looked. She was reading it!

"Hurry," Grandma said, and I threw the poster at Melanie, and Grandma pulled me into the balloon. I kind of fell on my head.

"Hey, Meg," Melanie said when I was in a pile on the floor of her balloon basket.

"Hey, Melanie," I said.

She was stoking the fire or whatever you do that makes the balloon float and was wearing a sweatshirt that said, *Follow your dreams, they know the way.* Her balloon team was holding ropes and waiting for her go-ahead. "I'm really excited to be a part of this," Melanie said.

This was unbelievable.

I was in a hot-air balloon.

My whole future was across a soccer field.

"Grandma. What are you doing? What are we doing?"

"Making history, my dear, making history."

I managed to stand up.

Dawn finished the excerpt and then the whole crowd looked over at us.

"Hit it!" Grandma yelled at Melanie, and Melanie revved the fire and motioned to her balloon people, and we floated up.

I grabbed the basket, my stomach dropping.

I had always wanted to go up in a balloon but not like this. NOT LIKE THIS.

Grandma took the Alzheimer's poster and held it up. "Smile," she said.

"They can't see my face, Grandma."

"Yes, they can. That's why we put on the makeup. Just smile and wave."

So I smiled and waved as we lifted up into the sky.

Grandma handed me the poster but I didn't know she was handing me the poster so I dropped it and we all watched as it floated down to the grass.

"Oh well," Grandma said to me.

Oh well? Oh well?!

"My name is Sally Stokes," Grandma said into the megaphone. "I am the proud grandma of this strong feisty determined young girl."

"We can't hear you," Dawn said over the PA.

The balloon was floating the wrong way. "Can you get the balloon over the stage?" Grandma asked Melanie, off megaphone.

"Sorry, I'm at the mercy of the wind and it just changed direction," Melanie Bacon said.

Oh. My. Gosh.

Grandma tried again, this time screaming into the megaphone. "MY NAME IS SALLY STOKES. I AM THE PROUD GRANDMA OF THIS STRONG FEISTY DETERMINED YOUNG GIRL."

It was no use.

We were over the trees now, floating up up up into the clouds and far far far away from the town of Jewel's 100th Strawberry Days annual Strawberry Pancake Breakfast.

20

Hot Air

And that is why I am declaring war on Grandma.

WAR!

She risked everything. Everything!

Can you imagine being in that strawberry, watching those beautiful bikes turn into specks on the horizon? Turn into dots of nothingness? Turn into far-off dreams you would never reach? While your entire town witnesses your downfall? Can you? Can you???

Some might say, *Meg. You* did *make history. Never before have two participants in the Strawberry Ambassador Competition floated into the atmosphere right before they were supposed to go on stage.*

Some might say, *Meg, the videos of you and your grandma waving in a giant strawberry went viral and people around the world are posting about it.*

Some might even say, *Meg, didn't your grandma promise to put on a show and didn't she follow through?*

All these things are true.

And because of these true statements, I am declaring war.

We had just flown away from the first event of the competition in a hot-air balloon.

We did, however, finish the speech.

Grandma said her part and then, I don't know why, but I said mine, all on the megaphone, over the side of the balloon to anyone who might be able to hear—the birds, a far-off airplane, and then of course Melanie Bacon, who put her hand over her heart by the time we were done.

"That was really good," Melanie said.

"Meg wrote most of it," Grandma said. "She's a fantastic writer."

"Thank you," I mumbled even though I was seething mad at her and determined to never speak to her again. Writers are suckers for compliments.

After that Grandma started talking with Melanie, who was very sorry that the wind was so unpredictable and Grandma was all, "Oh puffo! This is the best morning of my life!"

And that was when it really set in, really and truly set in. Best morning of her life?

I was fuming, billowing up in anger, and after the one

friendly exchange about my writing, I decided I would *really* not talk to her, not while I was boiling in utter despair.

So while we were flying and Grandma was talking to Melanie about how her family got into ballooning, I looked out on the town of Jewel. My town. My beautiful town, and I thought, *This day will never be forgotten by the citizens of Jewel.*

I also thought, *Being in a hot-air balloon is different than I'd imagined.*

I had never seen Jewel from the sky. I'd never seen anything from the sky, actually. There was a blanket of trees all different colors of green, like the quilts people sit on for picnics. There were also square and rectangle houses in between the trees, with cars that looked like tiny toys driving along.

The thing that made me almost gasp, but not loud enough for Grandma to hear because I was furious, was seeing the clear blue lake by our house.

I could see it!

And the tiny island in the middle where me and Hattie and Dad would sometimes go fishing. And if I squinted, our house. It was strange and kind of amazing to see it all from the clouds.

But of course, I was still mad and none of that mattered. But it was cool! How could I feel so many things at the same time?

Anyway, once we got on the ground and Melanie's balloon team met us with Melanie's balloon truck for the ride back to the park and we had to pack the whole thing up and it took pretty much our whole lives and I did not say one word the whole time, once all that happened and we were in the balloon truck Grandma said, "Meg, I know it didn't go as we planned, but I think it was still effective."

I folded my arms and looked out the window. There were cows.

"Why are you so upset?"

Lots of cows.

Grandma looked at Melanie, and Melanie looked at Grandma. Then Grandma looked at me again. "Meg, come on. It's not so bad."

"Grandma," I said, trying to keep my voice steady. I'd vowed not to talk to her, but this was getting ridiculous. "Not so bad? It's over. She's going to kick us out."

"Who's going to kick us out?"

"Dawn Allerton."

"Oh puffo."

"Oh puffo? Oh puffo? We just flew away from the breakfast!" My voice was no longer steady.

"It was fun! It added to the experience," Grandma said. "Melanie, don't you think so?"

Melanie nodded. She was driving the balloon truck right at the speed limit, I noticed. She's a very good driver of trucks and balloons if you ever want to go up in the strawberry balloon or ride in her truck. "I thought it was wonderful," Melanie said.

UGGGGGGHHH. Melanie knew Dawn Allerton. Everyone in Jewel knew Dawn. She was caving to Grandma.

"Grandma," I said, "Dawn will not tolerate what we just did. She's a rule follower and she's already mad at you because you yelled at her on the phone."

"I didn't yell at her. I talked to her sternly."

"You don't talk to Dawn Allerton sternly! You don't call the director of a major competition and tell them off! And you don't fly away right when you are supposed to give a speech! We're done. This is over because of you, Grandma. You ruined everything!"

Grandma looked shocked at my outburst. She really did, and why was it shocking? What did she think would happen? Wouldn't she say the same thing if she was me? Yes! She would!

"I am sorry that you think I ruined everything," she said in a teacher voice. She was treating me like one of her bad students. "But I'll have you know, I will talk sternly to whomever I want. And so will you. If you feel you've been treated unjustly you speak up. Also, this competition is not over for us. Nothing is ruined, okay, Meg? You got that? Life is not all or nothing. We'll just talk to her and it will be fine."

I shook my head. Unbelievable.

When we got to the park, the stage was taken down. The tables were gone. The chairs and the griddles and all the people had left. It was hard to imagine that just a few short hours ago, this has been the scene of my greatest humiliation.

Dawn was still there pacing around the parking lot with her assistant following her. When she saw us she stopped, her eyes looking like death.

"I told you. I told you!" I said.

Grandma looked at Dawn and took a deep long breath. Then she turned to me. "Don't worry. I'll handle it. She just needs a little honey."

Honey? What was she talking about? This was the fight of our lives, not an encounter with Pooh Bear.

We got out of Melanie's strawberry balloon truck.

Dawn marched toward us. "You're disqualified."

For once, I was upset that I was right.

Melanie Bacon came around and put her arm around me and I let her.

"I'm so sorry," she whispered.

I nodded. Willing myself not to cry.

"You don't need to disqualify us," Grandma said, standing straight, looking right into Dawn's eyes.

"Yes, I do," Dawn said, inches from Grandma.

Grandma did not back down.

"Why?"

"Because you didn't complete your speech and you left the venue and you, you, you ignored my instructions." She clapped her hands when she said that.

"Oh my," Grandma said. "Did you just clap your hands at me?"

"I did."

Grandma put fingers to her temples and I wondered if that was some kind of strategy. "I see that you are upset. My question is, didn't we make things more interesting for the crowd?"

Dawn's face got even redder. "It doesn't matter if the crowd was interested. You broke the rules."

That was when it occurred to me.

I put my hand on my stomach for bravery and spoke up. "Ms. Allerton," I said, stepping in front of Grandma and using my most respectful voice. "I am a longtime resident of Jewel."

"I know who you are, Meg Stokes."

Wow! She knew who I was? Even though she said it in a very irritated voice, this gave me a boost of confidence. "You do? Well, I know who you are and I admire you very much. I love what you've done with civic issues around here."

"Civic issues?"

Were those not the right words? Didn't *civic* mean *town*? Did I get it mixed up? "Um, I mean, I admire your principles and your passion for social, uh, justice?" *Keep going, Meg. Keep going.* "I thoroughly agreed with what you said about community when you came to speak at our school."

She narrowed her eyes. "Oh, that. Yes," she said. "That was an important speech for you young people to hear."

I nodded. "So important. Really important." I took a breath and kept going. "As you read in my essay, I am very passionate about civic, uh, responsibility and being a part of the community too. This festival is the most important thing I have ever taken part in. I am extremely serious about it."

I looked at my grandma. "As is my partner."

Grandma nodded and smiled big. Too big.

Dawn folded her arms, unconvinced, which I didn't blame her.

I kept going.

"I know what happened today was not, um, ideal."

"Not ideal?" Dawn said, exasperated.

"Right, right. We should have adhered to the instructions you gave us."

"Yes," Dawn said. "That's why you are disqualified."

I swallowed hard. "I understand. The thing is, we did technically give our speech."

"No, you didn't."

"We did. I have a witness." I looked at Melanie. "Melanie

Bacon, do you swear to tell the truth, the whole truth, and nothing but the truth?"

"What?" Melanie said.

"Can you be truthful?" I asked, trying to be very professional.

"Uh, yeah. Of course."

"Did we, or did we not, give our entire speech in your balloon?"

Melanie smiled and nodded. "They did. It was very touching."

"That doesn't . . ." Dawn started to say, but I interrupted. I had to. I really did.

"Sorry, Dawn, if you'll let Melanie finish. Did we or did we not give our full speech while we were still in Kiwanis Park airspace?" We were way up in the sky, but that park is big, and when I said the ending phrase of our speech— "Love conquers all, even in a little town called Jewel" were the exact words, if you want to know—I remember looking down and seeing the last bit of Kiwanis Park grass.

Melanie smiled. "You did!"

I nodded. "We did. And the rules specifically said to give a speech at Kiwanis Park and, well, we did that."

"She's right. We did," Grandma said.

Dawn stared at us. She was mad but she was faltering.

"Give us another chance," I said. "We will not

disappoint you again. I promise. You can give us some kind of consequence or punishment," I said. "Please, whatever you feel is fair, but technically, we should still be in this competition."

Dawn looked at her assistant. She looked at the balloon truck. She looked at the sky. Grandma nudged me and I was still very, very, VERY mad at her, but I allowed it.

Dawn said, "I'm warning both of you. One more thing like this and you're out."

I did it!

I was so excited I wanted to hug Grandma. Not really, but I wanted to hug someone. I should have hugged Dawn.

"We understand," I said. "Thank you. You will not be disappointed in this decision."

Dawn's nose twitched. "I'm already disappointed," she said.

"Oh, okay. Well, thank you."

She sighed. "Take this for tomorrow," Dawn said, handing us an envelope. "The rest of the groups will be starting the challenge at nine a.m. I am docking you a half hour because that's how much time I wasted talking to the crowd about your stunt."

"You talked about us flying away in a balloon for a half hour?" Grandma asked, but I said, "Perfect, thank you," and hurried Grandma away.

Dad and Hattie showed up just then. We'd called them

on Melanie's cellphone because Grandma had left hers in the truck.

"You guys," Dad said, once we were safely in the vehicle and away from Dawn, "that was amazing."

"No, it wasn't, Dad. We almost got kicked out," I said, my heart still racing from the encounter. I had just saved us from disqualification! I was relieved and kind of jumpy. I'd done it.

"You almost got kicked out?" Dad said, looking at me in the rearview mirror.

"Oh puffo. She was never really going to do it," Grandma said.

I looked at her, astounded. "Were you not there a few minutes ago?"

"I was and you did a marvelous job, my dear. Simply marvelous but I think that was all for show."

I was speechless.

"What happened?" Hattie asked.

Grandma then told the whole story, laughing about Dawn Allerton. "She was threatening to not let us compete. Can you imagine? But we called her bluff."

Called her bluff? She absolutely was serious. Absolutely.

Grandma glanced at me. "Wasn't this the best day? I can't wait to tell Grandpa about it."

I couldn't believe it. I really couldn't. She didn't understand the gravity of what had just transpired, what she had almost destroyed. This was a joke to her! And it was not a joke!

When we got home, I went straight up to my dad's loft and started writing this exposé.

I wrote:

> To Whom It May Concern:
> URGENT NEWS!!!!!!!!!
> My grandma is ruining my life and I am so mad I can hardly breathe.
> I am going to type everything that happens to me from here on out because I NEED THIS TO BE A MATTER OF PUBLIC RECORD!

I know you know I wrote that because you read it, but now you know why I wrote it and can you blame me? Can you?

Grandma is acting like this is a game.

This is not a game.

This is my life.

This is my freedom.

This is war.

21

War Is Declared!

After I started this exposé and Dad came up and tried to calm me down and sat in that dumb rocking chair and laughed at me, *laughed* at me, which was becoming all too common these days, and said things like, "Meg, you're being ridiculous. Are you really that mad at Grandma?"— after all that, and after Dad finally left me alone, I got the peace and quiet I needed to record everything that went down in the past few weeks.

It took forever.

Forever.

Then I opened the challenge envelope from Dawn Allerton *without Grandma* and read what the event was for tomorrow.

From now on, this was *my* competition. Grandma was going to be minimally involved—pretty much just a lady who stands near me while I do everything, if I could help it. It was the only way to win.

I read the challenge.

It wasn't so bad.

Actually, it was pretty easy, which I will tell you all about. But before that, and more importantly, in order to take back control of the competition and show Grandma that this kind of thing would not happen again—I would absolutely not let it happen again—I thought I should take a cue from the expert strategist in the field of war—my dad—and write an official declaration. Please file this in CLASSIFIED.

Dear Grandma,

I, Meg Amelia Stokes, officially declare war on you, Sally Margaret Stokes.

From here on out you can expect a hostile environment both in the house and at the competition.

I will be in charge of all challenges related to the Strawberry Ambassador Competition and I will be making every major decision.

I won't even let you read what we're supposed to do unless I decide I want to.

And I won't be wearing any costumes or makeup or anything else like that.

Sincerely,
Your Granddaughter,
Meg Amelia Stokes

"Hattie!" I yelled.

She came running up the stairs. "Can you deliver this to Grandma Sally?" I asked.

"What is it?"

"It's highly confidential pertaining to the ongoing competition and none of your business," I said in an official voice.

"That's rude," she said, and took the note.

She went downstairs. It was late afternoon and Mom had come home early. She had stuck her head up to see if I was okay and I said I was fine but that I was busy writing an exposé and she said, "Sounds good," and went back down.

She and Dad and Grandma Sally were in the kitchen talking and laughing. I could hear it like they were in the room with me, they were so loud.

But now Hattie was delivering a hefty blow in the form of a war declaration.

I waited to hear Grandma scream or for Dad to say, "No! Not again!" or for Mom to come storming up asking what had happened and if war was necessary.

It's necessary, Mom. It's necessary.

I waited.

And waited.

And waited.

"Hattie!" I yelled.

"What?" she yelled back.

"Come up here, I want to talk to you."

"I'm playing Karma with Grandma and Mom. Sorry."

They were playing cards??? And not just any cards, but my favorite game in the whole world?

"Hattie!" I yelled again.

"Come down and play," Mom called.

"No thank you, Mom." And then I said, "Did you hear what happened today with me and Grandma?"

"Yes!" she yelled back. "Were you scared?"

Are you kidding me?

"What? No. I was not scared."

I marched down the stairs. They were at the kitchen table. Dad too. THE WAR DECLARATION WAS THERE. OPENED. OUT FOR ALL TO SEE. DOING NOTHING. SITTING THERE LIKE A HAM SANDWICH.

"Hey, Meg," Mom said. "I can't believe you got to go up in a hot-air balloon with Melanie and Grandma. What an adventure."

An adventure?

"Want me to deal you in?" Dad asked.

"No way." He and Mom looked at me and they were suppressing smiles. I could see it. I could feel it. I did not appreciate it.

Grandma handed me a note, pleasant and calm, like she was inviting me to her birthday party. "This is for you."

I stormed back upstairs.

Dear Meg,

A war? I know that's what your dad resorted to. I was there. I lived it. I read the book. But, my dear grandchild, that was over a bedroom. This is a completely different situation. We are partners in a competition. This is no place for a war—if we are disharmonious we will fail. I am sorry if you didn't agree with my tactics today but we made a splash like we planned and excited the audience! Let's enjoy the experience, work together, and trust in love!

Xoxo
Grandma Sally

Oh no.

No.

No way.

Did she write that in the middle of her card game?

Just plop down the words *Enjoy the experience* about something that would profoundly change my daily life, and then draw a card?

I went back to my desk and started writing. Hard.

Grandma Sally,

We are at war whether you like it or not. The only way you end this is if you agree to do exactly what I say and let me be in charge because I am very passionate about this competition and I <u>live</u> in

Jewel so I know the rules better and also the town. The people around here appreciate in-depth speeches and historical facts much more than flashy outfits and lipstick. Also, I wrote the essay that got us in.

YOU ALMOST GOT US KICKED OUT TODAY!

From Your Granddaughter,
Meg Amelia Stokes

"Hattie!" I cried.

No response.

"Hattieeeeee!" I yelled even louder.

She stomped upstairs. "What? I'm about to win."

"Take this to Grandma."

She took the note. "This is dumb."

"Hattie," I said. "This is not dumb, this is my life, and yours if you want an electric bike."

Hattie's face changed. "Okay," she said. "Just don't be mean to her."

"I'm not being mean. I'm being stern. She says you can be stern to whoever you want if you feel you've been wronged."

Hattie nodded. "Okay, but Mom said to tell you to calm down." I did not love being told to calm down but at least Hattie took the note and left. I started pacing.

A few minutes later she was back with another note.

"Here," she said. She looked even more upset.

"What's wrong? Did you read it?"

"Huh? No. I just lost Karma. Grandma got me."

I shook my head. "You have to watch out for her, Hattie. She's not what she looks like on the outside. Beware!"

Hattie nodded and then went back downstairs.

Dear Meg,

    We are PARTNERS and while you do have a lot at stake in this competition, so do I and I will continue to compete. I'm a gal who loves a new experience and I can't wait to see what we get to do next. I also feel very passionate about the Alzheimer's Association, as you know. Most of all, I would like to grow closer to my grandchild and her family. Those are my goals. If you can't get on board, then we will have to find another solution. See you tonight at dinner!

                      Love, Grandma

I stared at it.

She was so cunning.

So clever.

So smart.

I wrote this:

Well then, if that's how you feel, I have no choice.
WAR!

I wrote it ten times and I highlighted it in yellow.

I called for Hattie and had it delivered. Then, when I was sure she'd had plenty of time to read it, I went downstairs.

They were still having a grand old time and all my war notes were piled up on the table.

"Dad. Can I use your cellphone?" I said.

"For what reason?"

"I want to talk to Lin."

I glanced at Grandma, who was either avoiding my look or studying her cards.

Dad handed me the phone. "What time do you guys need to be in town tomorrow?"

Grandma raised her eyebrows at me.

"You'll all find out when I decide you find out," I said, and then I stalked out of the room.

22

Second in Command

I called Lin's dad.

"Hello, Larry, can I please speak to Lin?"

"Yes, but I would like to tell you, that was the most delightful thing I have seen in a long time, Meg. You and your grandma working together to fly in a strawberry was genius."

"Thank you, Larry," I said in a professional voice. "Is Lin available?"

Lin got on. "Oh my gosh! You should have seen yourself."

"I know, Lin. I know."

"Are you okay? When did you get home? Was it amazing?"

I took a breath.

"I'm fine, but my grandma is out of control. And no, it

was not amazing," I said, even though parts of it were but the disqualification-undisqualification situation after was really not. "I have to do this thing by myself."

"What do you mean, by yourself?"

I told Lin about declaring war on Grandma. I told her that I was going to tell Grandma at *the last minute* what the challenges were and do all the prep work and make sure everything went exactly to my plan. "It's a war, Lin. I am giving her zero advantage."

Lin said she understood. "I can't believe Dawn Allerton almost cut you out of the competition."

"I can't believe she didn't," I said. "I saved our butts. We do have to start later than the others tomorrow as a penalty."

"What is the challenge?"

"I know what it is, but no one else in this house does, so I have to read it to you super quiet."

"That's fine. I have good hearing."

"That's true," I said. She once heard a dog barking a mile away, she told me.

"Okay, but first I have to ask you something and it's important."

"Sure," she said.

"I need you to take it seriously."

"Pinky swear."

I took a breath. "I don't know if I can trust anyone in

my house. It's really getting out of control over here and so . . . will you be my second in command?"

"What?"

"I need you to be my right-hand woman. I need you to be there for me and to be honest with me and to not let me down."

"Yes," she said. "I will," she said. "Anything you say," she added.

And *that's* the response of a true partner, so I read her the challenge.

STRAWBERRY AMBASSADOR FIRST EVENT

Strawberry Picking sponsored by Knudsen Strawberry Farms—

The Knudsen family has graciously invited us to pick strawberries on their UPICK acreage. The UPICK will be open for business for the public but they will have a section cordoned off specifically for the competition. That means there will be people there both picking and cheering you on. You and your partner will start picking at 9:00 a.m. You have until 4:00 p.m. to pick as many strawberries as you can. The partnership that picks the most will be awarded $1,000, care of Knudsen Strawberry Farms, to go to your charity. Those dollars will also be included

in your total for the grand prize. The team that
gets second place will receive $750, third place will
receive $500, fourth place will receive $250, and
last place will receive $100.
Please come ready to pick. This activity has been
happening in Jewel proper for over 100 years!
Happy harvesting!

Lin was quiet after I read it to her and then she said, "That seems really hard."

"All you have to do is pick strawberries."

"Have you ever gone strawberry picking before?"

"We have a strawberry patch in our front yard," I said. "I've picked tomatoes from our garden."

"This is a little different."

"I think it'll be fine."

"Are you sure?" Lin asked.

"Oh yeah. I mean, my plan is to pretty much sideline my grandma and do the whole thing myself."

"Really?"

I sighed. Lin didn't understand how serious I was about taking control. "Yes, really. I'm just going to bring her a juice or something and make her sit in the shade. She's not cut out for this stuff. She hasn't been preparing like I have."

"She didn't seem unprepared today," Lin said.

"Trust me. She is," I said.

Now you, reader, might be thinking the same thing as Lin. You might be thinking, *What are you talking about, Meg? Your grandma just ran across a field like a gazelle.*

I did write that Grandma was a gazelle and she really was for a few minutes, but what I failed to explain was that she was exhausted afterward. She kept saying to Melanie, "I'm exhausted." And when we got in the truck to ride home from the whole ordeal, she was snoring immediately, like right after she said that Dawn Allerton was bluffing, right after that she fell dead asleep and didn't wake up the entire ride home.

Me on the other hand, I was alert as a jaguar. I was quick as a skunk. I was wily as a coyote.

"I got this," I said to Lin.

"Okay," she said. "If you're sure."

"I'm sure," I said.

She offered to stop by at the strawberry fields and cheer me on, and I was very grateful to have at least one person on my side.

I was going to win the challenge.

I was going to take back the reins.

And things were going to go according to my plan.

Not Grandma's.

23

Only a Dope Will Mope

That night when Grandma came to get into bed, she had green stuff on her face and toilet paper all over her hair.

I wanted to ask what she was doing that for but also I didn't want to ask. Ever.

I was on the floor with a blanket and my pillow. I stared at the ceiling like a mannequin.

"You're sleeping down there?" she said in a weird voice. The green stuff was getting hard so she had to talk without moving her face, which seemed difficult, I have to say.

"I am."

"It will hurt your back sleeping on the hardwood like that," she said.

"I'll be fine, Grandma."

She sat on the bed. "You don't want to be sore tomorrow. Picking strawberries is hard work."

I looked at her. "How did you know we were picking strawberries?" I'd put the competition envelope under my dresser.

She held up her phone. "It's posted on the Strawberry Days website. They're putting up the challenges by seven each night."

"What? When did they say that?"

"Your dad said they announced it at the breakfast. I guess it was after we flew into the cosmos."

I clenched my teeth.

She took off her slippers. "So you're really doing this war thing?"

I took a moment. Then, because I had researched and found tips from a well-known resource called *The Art of War* while they were all playing card games and not focusing on the competition, I found out that you have to be disciplined as a leader on the battlefield and you have to have high standards for yourself and also for the people you are in charge of (this was complicated because I was both in charge of Grandma and at war with her). I said, "We are doing this war. Thank you for asking, Grandmother."

She sighed. "I just don't think it's for the best, Meg. Forgiveness is the way forward."

I smiled and turned to her. "Okay, Grandma. I forgive you. Now will you do everything I say?"

She laughed. "I will not."

"Then it's war."

Hattie walked in. She had green stuff on her face and toilet paper in her hair! I wasn't sure what they were doing but it made me feel kind of bad that while I was upstairs getting ready for the next challenge they were downstairs hanging out and putting stuff on their faces and wasting toilet paper without me.

"Are you guys fighting?" Hattie asked.

"No," Grandma said.

"Yes," I said.

Grandma sighed. "I picked out clothes for both of us for the strawberry picking."

I looked at her. She what?

"They're laid out on the couch. We need to get to the UPICK early even if we can't start right away so we can see what the layout is."

"It's a field of strawberries, Grandma."

She nodded. "I realize that but nonetheless, I'd like to get there and be ready to go. We should make lunches and take snacks."

I could not believe how she was being. *I* was going to say we should make lunches and bring snacks. *I* was in charge. My mind started working fast. I had to stop this. I had to make a move.

"Water is what we need," I said. "That's number one what we need."

"Yes. Of course." She got in bed.

"You should be nice to Grandma," Hattie said.

I didn't say anything because there was nothing to say. I rolled over and just as I was about to fall asleep, a war idea sprang to life.

"See you in the morning. I think we should go for a fresh start, Meg. That's what I think," Grandma said.

I was silent as a snake and then she turned out the lights.

"You know, Meg," she said, "only a dope will mope."

24

Night Attack

First act of war.

At three in the morning my watch vibrated. Following in my dad's footsteps when he had a war with his grandpa, I felt like the middle of the night was the best time to get things done.

I got up.

Grandma's CPAP machine was humming.

Hattie was snoring.

Conditions were perfect.

I tiptoed out to the front room and found the clothes Grandma had laid out on the couch. She had my flannel shirt THAT I WORE IN THE WINTER. A T-shirt. Long jeans. My leather boots and a big old fat sun hat. For her she had overalls, one of my mom's flannel shirts, a T-shirt, and boots. There were heavy socks for both of us and scarves and gloves.

I couldn't believe it.

Did she think we lived in the Arctic? It was supposed to be ninety-nine degrees tomorrow. If we wore all this we would die of heatstroke.

I gathered everything up and made my way outside to the shed.

It was stuffed with Dad's boxes. They were stacked all over the place; some of them looked like they were about to fall over.

I took both our flannel shirts and flung them as far back into the shed as I could. They slid down behind the boxes! Score! Then I threw the jeans and the overalls, which didn't slide all the way down but far enough. I put each boot in a different box and chucked the scarves and gloves over by the rakes.

I was about to put the socks in a bag of compost when I heard a noise.

I stopped.

Something was moving.

I held my breath.

A cracking sound. Like a piece of wood breaking.

Goose bumps rose on my arms. It was dark out, not even the moon and everything quieter than usual, except those sounds, that crack.

The trees were looming, there were shadows, and I felt like I was being watched—I could feel a prickling all over my skin.

I slowly, slowly, slowly turned around.

Eyes! Eyes staring at me! Eyes of darkness!

I muffled a scream and staggered backward and was about to be attacked when I realized what it was.

A fox.

I let out a breath.

"You scared me," I said, my heart thumping.

The fox didn't move.

"I'm just hiding her stuff," I whispered. "It's an act of war. She'll get it all back."

The fox still didn't move.

"Shoo," I said. "Shoo. Go away."

Nothing. The goose bumps came back. Did Grandma send the fox? Did she and her adventure friends study spells along with upcycling and scuba diving?

Oh, whatever. I threw everything left into the shed as fast as I could and then I ran to the house.

"Leave me alone, fox. It's not my fault," I hissed.

I opened the door, tripped over a box and a Frankenstein mask, and almost yelled out in pain.

Almost.

Almost.

But, like a real war leader, I enacted my incredible

self-control and discipline and made no sound at all. Instead I crawled wounded to my bed on the hardwood floor of my room, Grandma and Hattie sleeping away.

"Strike one, Grandma. Your spooky fox didn't scare me."

Meg 1, Grandma 0

25

Strategy and Supplies

The next morning I woke up to the sweet sound of Grandma saying, "Stephanie, did you move our clothes?"

I sat up.

"What clothes?" Mom asked.

"I put out those clothes for Meg and me for the competition today."

"No," Mom said. "Nothing was out here when I got breakfast."

Grandma started walking back to the room and I hit the deck and acted like I was sleeping.

I heard her come in.

I heard her watch me.

I heard her feel the pain of war.

I held very still like a piece of wood.

She left.

I heard her ask Dad.

I heard her ask Hattie.

I stayed in my sleeping bag laughing in my heart.

When it was almost time to go, I got up and put on a tank top and a pair of cut-offs. Grandma hadn't come back in the room.

I went to the kitchen and she and Hattie and Dad were eating cereal. Grandma was wearing a T-shirt, another one of Mom's long-sleeved flannel shirts, some jeans, and a pair of tennis shoes. She had a bandana around her neck and Mom's beach hat on her head. She picked up her orange juice and drank it without looking at me.

Why was she wearing the hottest clothes possible? Was she worried an unexpected blizzard would move in today?

"How'd you sleep, Meg?" Dad asked.

"Fine." I sat down and poured some cereal.

"We need to get going," Grandma said. She didn't say anything about my clothes. Instead she handed me some sunscreen. "Put some of this on."

I looked at her. "I already put some on in the bathroom."

"What's the SPF?"

I had no idea but I said, "One thousand."

Dad looked at me. "Meg. Come on."

Grandma smiled. "We'll get over this. Don't worry, Peter."

Grandma went to call Grandpa Arthur to check in.

I got my lunch ready and put in like fifteen Double Stuf

Oreos for energy, a root beer, a handful of corn chips, half a grapefruit, a hard-boiled egg I found in the back of the fridge, and some Swedish Fish. I put my lunch sack in a string backpack I got free at the movie theater once. An abundance of supplies is key to keeping warriors refreshed and energized. I added in another Oreo.

I called Lin to tell her that I was prepared and to find out what time she was coming. Then Grandma got her lunch ready while I looked for my baseball hat and Hattie was singing a Beatles song called "Strawberry Fields" really loud and Dad said, "Hattie, please."

I kept forgetting things like my ChapStick, my sunglasses, and a good-luck stone duck that I won at Strawberry Days two years ago that I try to keep in my pocket at all times.

Grandma kept yelling, "Meg, we're going to be late!"

And I kept yelling, "We don't get to start until ninethirty!"

And she kept yelling, "I told you I wanted to get there early!"

And I kept yelling, "We have tons of time!"

Finally, we were in the truck. Dad was going to drop us off and then come back and pick us up at the end of the day.

"You aren't going to watch us?"

"I want to but I have to work."

"Really?"

"Sorry, Megs. Mom and Hattie and I will all be there at the end to see you win, though."

I looked at Grandma. She had a gigantic backpack— like one you would take to the Alps—sitting next to her.

"Are you going to carry that around with you?"

"I'm bringing it just in case. I also have a hydration bladder for both of us."

I held up my water bottle. "I'm fine."

Grandma nodded. "Great."

26

Strawberry Fields Forever

The fields were past Lin's house on the outskirts of town. They were part of the biggest strawberry farm in the county.

Everyone from the competition was standing around at the barn, and there were people who weren't in the competition too. They took pictures of Grandma and me when we got out of the monster truck.

"See, Meg? We're famous."

"Yay," I said, acting annoyed, but I did do a pretty good face for the cameras.

Dawn Allerton and her assistant were both wearing sun visors and business suits. There was a lady with a cowboy hat who I guessed was the person in charge of the UPICK. Dawn Allerton was reading her clipboard and then looked up at us.

"Ah, Meg and Sally Stokes are finally here."

"Are we late?" Grandma asked, looking at her watch.

"No, but everyone else was early."

Grandma gave me a look.

I folded my arms like I didn't care but I did care. I couldn't let the war with Grandma distract me. I couldn't get lazy. Those bikes were my ticket to happiness.

The lady with the hat was named Norma Knudsen. She and her family had been running these fields for over fifty years.

Everyone clapped.

"Thank you, thank you very much," she said. Then she told us how to pick:

> Look for berries that are entirely red, plump, and firm. They don't ripen once they're picked.

> Cradle the fruit in your hand. (Diego laughed at this, I don't know why.) Pinch the stem off with your thumb and forefinger and gently put it in your container.

> Don't stack the strawberries too high or they will damage the ones below.

> Once your crate is filled, move it to the shade. Strawberries don't last long in the hot sun.

> Be careful not to step on the plants or damage them as you move up and down the rows.

Picking ended at four and we were to then bring our strawberries to the weighing station to find out who won.

There were bleachers set up by the weighing station for spectators.

"We'll be the winners today, my friends," Diego said to me and Ellie.

"No, you won't," Ellie said.

"We probably will be. My brother does like a hundred burpees a day," he told Ellie.

"Burpees?" Ellie asked.

"Shhhhhh. Be respectful of Norma Knudsen, please. Or I'll assign even more time penalties," Dawn Allerton said.

We stopped talking but Diego kept raising his eyebrows and it was annoying. Just because his brother could do burpees didn't mean he'd be good at picking strawberries.

"Take breaks when you need to," Norma Knudsen said.

"I won't need a break but I was thinking maybe you should sit this one out to be ready for the next challenge," I whispered to Grandma.

"You'll need breaks," Grandma whispered back.

"No, I won't," I said.

"And make sure to eat lunch and stay hydrated," said Norma Knudsen. Then she handed out crates for us to fill and showed us where to put them in the shade once they were at capacity.

"Hey," Diego said as we walked toward the field. "Did

you guys get a time penalty? Is that what Allerton was talking about?"

"We have to start a half hour late but it's fine. I'm really good at picking strawberries."

He nodded. "Me too." Then he said, "Your grandma is dressed like Paul Bunyan."

"She's Paula Bunyan to you," I said.

He smirked. "I have to say, the odds are not in your favor."

"Oh, really? Who won the math tournament?"

"You barely won. Barely. And this is not math."

"Well, who did the most online assignments last year?"

I really killed it at online school, I have to say.

"Meg, first of all, you did things that we didn't need to do. You're a pleaser, Meg, and life isn't about pleasing, it's about maximizing your time and winning."

Oh my gosh. Diego was the worst.

"And second of all, those have nothing to do with what you see before you." He waved his hand toward the enormous strawberry fields. "You and your grandma are at an extreme disadvantage and it makes me sad because usually you put up such a great fight."

I burned. I burned! "How dare you!" I said. "I don't fight, I win."

He smiled and walked over to his brother.

How was I going to do this? My grandma on the one hand and Diego (and all the other competitors) on the other. It was very draining.

At nine a.m., Dawn said, "Pickers, please go to your positions."

Diego and Ellie and Cooper and Zoe and all of them lined up at a row of strawberries. Diego looked over and tipped his hat.

"I really like Diego," Grandma said. "He seems kind-hearted." We were sitting on chairs in the shade of the farmhouse, where I hoped Grandma would stay the whole dang day. I didn't want to deal with her passing out on top of everything else.

"He's not kindhearted, Grandma. He's the enemy."

"I thought *I* was the enemy."

I sighed. "You both are."

"On your mark," Dawn said. I sat on the edge of my seat. "Get set." I wished so badly I was out there. I was going to have to make up so much time. "Go!"

Everyone started picking. The energy was palpable.

Not really.

It kind of was but then they were just picking strawberries. They were all bent down and going so slow. Why weren't they going faster?

"They're going to be sore later," Grandma said.

"What do you mean?" I asked her.

"We have to protect your back. You squat down and

you pick as low as you can. If that gets too hard, you have to get on your knees."

Protect your back? Get on your knees?

She handed me some gloves. "Use these."

"I don't want to," I said. "It's too hot."

"Meg," she said. "Please."

I sighed and took the gloves.

Right before nine-thirty I turned to Grandma. "Listen," I said. "I release you."

"You what?"

"I release you. You don't have to pick strawberries. I'll do enough for the both of us."

"What are you talking about? Of course I'm going to pick. Wear your gloves."

"Grandma," I started to say, but then Dawn announced it was time. "Okay, ladies, you're up."

I ran to our row.

Grandma walked behind me. Slowly. Like an anteater.

And so it began.

27

Good Luck

It turns out picking strawberries is the hardest thing in the history of the world.

I went fast at first.

Really fast, I think.

I was pulling those babies off their stems, moving like a ninja and squatting how Grandma said to instead of bending my back. I was smart enough to recognize sage advice when I heard it—though I would never tell Grandma that.

That was the first five minutes.

I was ahead of Grandma, who was on the other side of the row and way behind me.

After five more minutes, my thighs were burning and my back was starting to ache and I was sweating like crazy.

I took a break and drank some water.

Diego and Ellie and Cooper and Zoe were ahead of us but not as far as I thought they'd be. Everyone seemed to be moving in slow motion. The plants were low to the ground and there was no easy way to do it.

Grandma passed me and looked over. "You okay?"

"I'm fine. I'm just getting a drink."

She nodded. "That's good. Drink all you can."

Then she kept picking.

I picked too but the squatting was getting impossible, so I decided to go on my knees like she told me. Then I kind of crawled like a slug. Or a cougar, more like. Do cougars crawl? Anyway, I was crawling and picking and the sun was beating down and after a couple of hours, I had to lie down. I lay in the dirt.

Grandma was clear down the row. Like half a football field away.

She was past every single other person out there. Even Zoe and her dad, who had been in the lead.

Diego and Cooper and Ellie were all crawling like me. Zoe was squatting like Grandma and so was her dad, but they were barely moving and kept sitting down to rest.

The worst part was that I was cooking like bacon. My skin felt like it was on fire.

So I lay down. Just to rest for a minute.

"Meg!" someone yelled. It was Lin. She was calling from outside the cordoned section.

I got up and walked over; my legs felt like lead and I was only on my second crate. Grandma had four over in the shade.

"What are you doing?"

"I'm picking strawberries."

"You were just lying in the dirt."

Well, that was a rude thing for a second in command to say.

"Look, the sun is killing me."

Lin crossed her arms. "Why are you wearing a tank top? You have to cover up when you do field work or you burn and die."

I stared at her. "Says who?"

"Says all people. I've picked raspberries with my cousins, and if you don't cover up, you get cooked."

"Why didn't you tell me?"

"I thought everyone knew." We looked at Diego, who was sitting there. He waved at us. Ellie did too. They were both wearing T-shirts.

"I guess not many people know."

"Should I go get you a long-sleeved shirt?"

I shook my head. "We can't have outside help."

"Oh. That's dumb."

Then we both looked at Grandma clear down the field. "Wow," Lin said.

"I know," I said. "She's really good."

"That's 'cause she's experienced," Lin said. "I talked to my mom about what you said, how your grandma was going to be bad at this? And she said we'd be surprised. She said people like your grandma know how to work harder than us. Our generation is lazy."

Did that light a fire under my bum or what. "That's not true." I looked at Grandma plugging along out in the field.

Lin shrugged.

Ugh. I needed to get back out there and show everyone that I could work as hard as my grandma. "I have to go," I said.

"Good luck!" Lin said, and for the first time, I felt like I needed it.

28

Little Women

I picked really hard for another twenty minutes, I swear, but then I had to lie down again. It was impossible.

I stared at the sky. Why was this so difficult? Why was my life turning out this way? Why couldn't I go on?

I sat up.

I ate a strawberry.

Then I ate another one.

They were really good.

So then I was just sitting there eating strawberries.

Finally Grandma came over.

"What do you think you're doing?"

"I'm eating strawberries."

She put her hands on her hips. "You're getting burned."

"No, I'm not."

"Yes, you are."

I lay back down in the dirt and curled up in a ball.

She stood there towering over me, which I kind of liked because she was giving me shade.

Then she squatted down. "You have to stop this. Get up and start picking. We're going to lose."

"I know," I said. "It's just so hot."

"You need more clothes."

I didn't say anything because I did need more clothes and I was out of water and also because there was nothing to say.

"I thought this might happen. I brought some extra. They're in my backpack. Go change and then I'll help you fill your crate."

"Thanks, Grandma."

I was embarrassed but also relieved.

I walked all the way back down the row to the starting point. People were gathered weighing strawberries and talking to Norma, who waved to me.

"How are we doing?" she called.

"Fantastic," I said.

I found Grandma's backpack and took it in the bathroom, which was really small with only two stalls and not the best place to change clothes.

I waited until it was empty and opened Grandma's backpack.

There was some blue fabric. Probably a shirt.

I started to pull it out.

And pull it out.

And pull it out.

Finally, the entire thing was out of the backpack. I have no idea how she got it all in there.

It was a dress.

A *gigantic* dress.

Like a huge, bright blue, full-skirt, gigantic dress from some old-fashioned play. *Oklahoma!? Pioneer Town? Large Dress Play?*

I stared at it.

It was puffy sleeved.

It went to the ground.

There was a weird slip sewn in that made the skirt a big circle.

There was also a bonnet.

This wasn't extra clothes in case I needed them.

This was an act of war.

I seethed.

I distinctly said NO COSTUMES.

Grandma was fighting nasty.

I opened the bathroom door. "Lin!" I yelled. She was talking to some lady by the weighing station.

"Lin!" I yelled again.

She didn't hear me.

I cleared my throat, "LIN!!!!!"

She looked at me. The lady looked at me. All the straw-berry pickers looked at me. Dawn Allerton looked at me.

She'd been sitting under a shade tent with her assistant and now she was standing up. "Is there something wrong, Ms. Stokes?" she asked.

Lin was walking over.

"No," I said.

Dawn looked at Lin. "You can't have assistance from spectators."

"I know," I said. "I just need to talk to her real quick."

Dawn Allerton gave me a serious look.

I tried to give her a very nice I'm-doing-nothing-wrong look back. I don't think it worked but I pulled Lin into the bathroom anyway.

"What's wrong?"

I showed her the dress.

"What is that?" she said in awe.

"My grandma said she brought extra clothes for me to pick in."

Lin covered her mouth. "Are you serious?"

"Yes."

We held it up. "Wow. It's incredible," Lin said. She was not focusing. Not at all.

"What am I going to do?"

Lin put it under her chin. "You'd be covered." She touched the weird lace collar at the neck. "It's so beautiful."

I balled my fists. "I can't do this. If I back down now, I'll lose all credibility."

Lin looked at me in the mirror. "This is for the Leaf bikes, Meg. Think about the Leaf bikes. Think of us at the pool all summer. The frozen lemonades. The movies."

"I know, but Lin, I can't let her win. I can't."

Lin sighed. "Your grandma is kicking strawberry butt out there and it's because she's wearing the right clothes . . . and because she's experienced."

"I know," I said. I'd made a mistake chucking all those clothes in the shed. A terrible mistake.

"At least try it on."

I sighed. "Fine."

Lin pulled it over my head.

I wiggled out of my shorts and yanked it down over my body and then she tied the bow in the back.

I put on the bonnet.

I even put on the bloomer things that went under the skirt.

When I was all dressed Lin said, "It's amazing."

"No, it's not." I was a lady of the plains from some boring movie.

"I love it," she said.

"Lin! You're my second in command. You're supposed to help me."

"I *am* helping you! It's so gorgeous and it will cover up your skin from the sun."

She stood behind me looking into the mirror.

"I'm not doing it."

A lady walked in and said, "Oh my. Is there some kind of performance today?"

"Yes," Lin said.

"How fun," she said, and went into a stall.

Lin looked at me, smiling.

"Would you please go get my grandma?"

29

A Dirty Trick

Grandma Sally walked into the bathroom and clapped her hands in joy. "That's my Little Woman! That's it!" Uggghhhhhhhhh.

"Grandma," I said. "I will not."

"It's perfect. You'll feel so much better."

Lin leaned against the wall, grinning her face off, and the lady who'd asked if I was doing a performance came out of the stall and said, "Oh! You're the two from the strawberry thing! I didn't recognize you," she said to me. "But I sure do recognize you!" she said to Grandma.

Awesome.

"Well, thank you," Grandma said.

The lady was clearly thrilled as she vigorously washed her hands. "I was wondering what stunt you'd pull today!

I can't wait to tell my husband. It's perfect," she said, nodding at me and my large dress that I would never ever wear outside the confines of this bathroom.

"We think so," Grandma said.

I cleared my throat. "Would it be all right if we have the bathroom to ourselves? My grandmother and I have a couple things to discuss."

"Yes," Grandma said. "And we're losing precious picking time."

Lin gave me a thumbs-up as they left, which I did not appreciate.

Once they were gone, I turned to Grandma. "I said no costumes."

"This isn't a costume. This is a dress my friend Susan made for fun." She considered this and then said, "But they did use it in *Little Women* back in 2011."

"I'm not wearing it. I said no costumes and I meant it."

"Fine," Grandma huffed. She started to leave.

"Wait," I said. "We have to finish this together."

"You asked for my help and I gave it. I'm not going to sit around here and argue, goose."

I sighed. I couldn't go back out there, not in the blazing sun and get dried out like a potato chip, but I wasn't giving up. "There's got to be something else we can do."

She looked at me. "Well." She folded her arms. "I have one idea, but I don't think you'll like it."

"What? I'll do whatever as long as it doesn't involve a costume."

"Will you?"

"Please."

"Fine," she said, picking up her gigantic backpack. "Get your clothes back on and then I'll help you."

"Okay."

As I went into the stall she said, "Just remember, you did this to yourself."

I did this to myself.

Stay strong, Meg. Stay strong.

I changed back into my tank top and shorts.

When I came out, Grandma was waiting with a roll of toilet paper.

I looked at her. "What's that for?"

"Sun protection."

"Toilet paper isn't supposed to see the sun," I said.

"Toilet paper is meant to withstand a lot," she said, giving me a wink.

My heart sank.

"Really?"

"You said you'd do anything. If it's good enough for my hair, it's good enough for your arms and legs."

"Grandma," I said.

"Hurry up, sis."

I walked over. "How will it stay on?"

"Medical tape." And of course, she'd packed a first-aid kit.

So Grandma wrapped my arms, my legs, my neck, and part of my head.

"You don't have to do my head, Grandma, I have a hat."

"Oh puffo. We're going the whole hog if we're going at all." She was a toilet paper wizard, it turns out.

"It's not going to stay on," I said.

"Sure, it will," she said, taping on one more piece. She packed the roll back into the backpack for safekeeping and smiled at me. "Let's go get 'em, mummy" was the last thing I heard before she went out the door.

Point Grandma.

Meg 1, Grandma 1

30

Grandma Strikes Again

I made my way outside.

Was it hard to walk? Yes.

Did the paper rip? A little, but not as much as I thought it would. Like I said, Grandma was an excellent toilet paperer.

Did people stare? Uh, yes, they did.

When we walked out, Dawn Allerton looked confused, but she didn't say anything. There were no explicit rules against taping toilet paper all over your body.

Diego and everyone else stopped picking and watched as we walked over to our strawberry crates.

A kid over in the public section started crying.

"That's not a real mummy, honey," his mom said. "That's a girl."

Great.

But I wasn't going to lose so I took deep breaths, knelt next to Grandma, and started picking,

I have to say, I felt better.

I really did.

I picked and picked and when the paper ripped too much, Grandma taped me back together.

After a while, from three rows back, Diego called, "Why are you toilet papered?"

"None of your business!" I yelled back.

"It helps with the sun," Grandma called.

What the heck!

Soon Diego went to the bathroom and came back with toilet paper wrapped around his arms and legs. "There's tape in my backpack," Grandma said.

"They're our enemies."

"Oh puffo," she said. "We're all here for good causes. Besides, you put out love and love comes back to get you."

If she weren't such a fast picker, I'd say she was the worst competitor in history.

Around one, Dawn Allerton rang a bell. "Break for lunch!"

Everyone stood up, exhausted.

I stood up too. Grandma did not.

"Grandma, it's lunch," I said.

She didn't stop.

"Grandma." I walked over to her. "It's time to stop."

"I'm going to keep going."

"You are?"

"Yep."

"But you said to take breaks and we have to eat."

"I have been stopping every fifteen minutes for a drink and a handful of nuts. I have my sun hat and my gloves, and I've been pacing myself. I have plenty of energy. Plus we took all that time off to discuss that Little Woman dress." She sat back on her haunches. "And I brought a portable lunch."

She really was a hard worker.

"You're not going to go sit at those tables?" I asked, pointing at the bright red luxurious wooden picnic tables over in the shade of a large fluffy tree, where everyone was relaxing and laughing. Diego and Dan were already sprawled out on the grass picking off toilet paper and sipping Gatorade.

"Nope," Grandma said. "You can go on ahead. I'll keep working."

I thought about my Oreos, my egg, my root beer.

"I might just go over for a bit."

"Fine by me, soldier," she said.

That stung. It really stung. Today was not my day.

"I would keep working but I need to eat, and I don't

have a portable lunch or whatever." I had no idea what that was.

"Oh well, if you want to keep going, I brought enough for you."

My heart was breaking into a thousand pieces. "You did?"

"Yup. I want to win, so I came prepared. Go get my backpack."

I sighed. Were there more things in that never-ending backpack?

And yes, there were more things in the backpack. At the bottom of the bag were two hats. Each hat had a cup on top with a straw coming down. "This way we can pick and eat at the same time," Grandma said. She got out a thermos and poured green thick liquid into the cups on the hats.

"What is that?"

"Power smoothie. I'd put it in the hydration bladders but we need to still drink water while we eat. I saw these hats in the costume boxes when Grandpa and I were load-ing up to come here. I found them this morning while you were sleeping in."

I wasn't sleeping in. I was lying on the hardwood floor thinking I had outsmarted my grandma.

She handed me a hat with a cup filled with green sludge. I put it on.

"There's a buckle," she said.

"A buckle?"

"Yup. To keep the drink from falling."

I buckled it. Right under my toilet paper chin.

Meg 1, Grandma 2

31

Strawberry Fields for Never

We drank lunch.

And drank water.

We picked strawberries.

Grandma taped on more toilet paper when needed.

And Grandma stuck with me so that we were picking together. I told her not to.

"Grandma, just go ahead. It doesn't make sense."

She put three strawberries in my basket.

"Meg. Do you think I'm here to win fastest strawberry picker?"

"Uh, yes, Grandma. That's exactly why you're here."

"Nope." She picked three more strawberries. I was sitting on my butt giving her my full attention and wiping the sweat off my smoothie hat brow. "I'm here because I love you."

No.

No.

No.

"Grandma. We're not here for love. We're here to win."

Grandma smiled. SHE SMILED.

"I'm serious, Grandma. I'm dead serious. That's why I declared war. I can't have you taking off in hot-air balloons and going slow on purpose and kneeling here talking about love. I want to win."

"I know," Grandma said. "I understand. I think we have a good chance. I'm just telling you, I will try hard, but my priority is you."

"Nope," I said. "This is what I was worried about." I was about to say something profound about Grandma Sally's attitude but then a bee landed on my face and I screamed, and it flew away.

"Whoops," Grandma said, and kept picking.

So I gave up.

The afternoon wore on.

Some people surged, like Zoe and her dad, who took the quickest lunch and were pretty close behind us. Other people faltered, like Mr. Bailey and Cooper, who kept going to sit under the lunch tree, or Ellie and her mom, who left for three hours to do who knows what.

Grandma told me stories.

She told me about riding her bike barefoot down an old highway, screaming at the top of her lungs when she was my age.

"Why didn't you wear shoes?"

"It was summer," she said, like that was an obvious answer.

I told her about finally learning to do a front flip off the diving board at the swimming pool last July when I went for Lin's birthday.

"Was it scary?" she asked.

"Kind of. But I liked it."

She laughed. "That's the best kind of scary."

She told me about working in the cannery when she was a teenager. "Fastest canner in the county."

"Like you put stuff in cans?"

"Yup. Beans. Corn. Peaches. You name it."

I had never thought about how food got inside cans on the shelf at the store. I also had no idea my grandma was a part of that.

I told her how I threw up after riding the white roller coaster at Lagoon with my friends. "It was so embarrassing."

"Eh," Grandma said. "Everyone vomits. They'll forget."

She told me about picking strawberries growing up with her best friend Tootsie. No wonder she knew what she was doing.

"Tootsie? Her name was Tootsie?"

"Her name *is* Tootsie. She lives in New York. I'll have you meet her sometime."

I told her that Lin was my best friend and that she was over there eating Popsicles with Diego. Hey!

"Lin!" I yelled.

She waved. "Come get one."

I looked at Grandma. "Can I?" I asked.

We had by far the most strawberries and there was only forty-five minutes left.

"Up to you," she said.

"Do you want one?"

"No thanks," she said.

I took off my smoothie hat. "I'll be fast," I said, and ran over.

When I got to Lin and Diego they were both clapping. "You win this one," Diego said. "You guys are doing way better than us."

"Thank you," I said. I bought a Popsicle from the refreshment stand. "What can I say. She's a strawberry picker."

"No kidding," Diego said. "Me and Dan are hoping for third."

Dan came out of the bathroom and bought a Popsicle too.

We talked for a bit.

Then Dan said, "We should probably get back. It's almost four."

"What?" I looked at my watch. Had we been standing here that long?

Lin gasped.

"What's wrong?"

She pointed. "What is she doing?"

We all looked.

Grandma was over by Zoe and her dad and she was pouring our strawberries into their crates!

I REPEAT: SHE WAS POURING OUR STRAWBERRIES INTO THEIR CRATES!

"No!" I cried, and started running.

Diego and Dan were right behind me.

"Grandma!" I yelled.

She didn't stop.

More strawberries and more.

When I got there half our last crate was gone, there were strawberries smashed on the ground, Zoe was crying and laughing, and her dad was saying, "Sally. This is too much."

That was when Dawn rang the bell to end the competition.

32

The Bitter Results

Everyone was staring at Grandma and Zoe and Zoe's dad.

"What's going on?" I said, trying to catch my breath.

"Zoe had a little accident," her dad said. "She tripped and a bunch of our strawberries fell and got smashed."

Zoe wiped her eyes. "I'm the worst."

"Don't say that," Grandma said. "It was an accident."

Dawn Allerton walked up then. "Good job, all of you. It was a long day."

We'd had so many strawberries and now it looked like we had about the same as Zoe. The same! After all that. I looked at Diego's and Dan's and they had a lot too. Had my grandma just thrown the challenge?

"How could you do that?" I whispered.

"We'll still win," she said.

"Are you sure?"

"Of course. Our crates are loaded with a lot more strawberries. Besides, the poor thing was hysterical. You would have done the same thing."

"No. No, I wouldn't."

One by one, Dawn called each team up to weigh their strawberries. The bleachers were filled with people watching.

Dad yelled, "Go, Mom! Go, Meg!" He stood up and did a weird raise-the-roof thing that he does. Mom was clapping, Hattie was cheering. My heart was a black hole.

First up were Ellie and her mom, who had only a few crates.

They weighed Cooper and Mr. Bailey's next. They had more crates but theirs weighed barely more than Ellie and her mom. There was no way to know who had more because we all filled our boxes differently.

Next they weighed Diego and Dan's. As they lugged their crates over to the scale, all my confidence went down the drain.

"Grandma," I whispered again. "They're going to beat us."

"No. They're not."

They weighed Dan and Diego. The scale needle shot up. Grandma went white.

Diego yelled, "That's right!"

Dan was laughing. "Holy cow, we got a ton."

Norma Knudsen looked at Dawn. "Those are some loaded boxes of strawberries."

Diego smiled at me.

I folded my toilet paper arms. *Please please please.*

Zoe and her dad went next. "Thank you so much for your help," Zoe said to Grandma.

"Of course," Grandma said, but she didn't seem as cheery.

They put the strawberries on the scale and the needle went almost to the top—past Diego and Dan's record. My heart was now the deepest and blackest of holes.

"Wow!" Norma Knudsen said. "I've never seen two amateur pickers get that many strawberries."

Zoe whooped. Her dad laughed and gave her a hug.

Then it was our turn.

I looked at Dad, who was standing with his hands to his mouth. Mom gave me a thumbs-up.

I closed my eyes. *Please please please.*

"Okay, here we go," Norma Knudsen said, "last but not least, Sally and Meg Stokes."

She put the strawberries on the scale.

There was a gasp.

I opened one eye.

Diego's mouth hung open.

Zoe was staring at me, clutching her dad's hand.

The needle went high but not high enough.

Second place.

Second.

33

Second Is the First Loser

I was livid.

Boiling.

Flames.

Flames.

Flames.

Even Grandma seemed upset.

"Is that right?" she asked.

Norma Knudsen nodded. "The scale doesn't lie."

Zoe's dad, he said, "I think maybe, um, we should give some of our strawberries back to the Stokes team."

"Nope," Dawn Allerton said, too quickly. "No way. The results are final." She looked at me and Grandma. "We make choices every day, don't we, ladies. And we must live by our choices."

For some reason, this emboldened Grandma or what-ever. Before Dawn said that, she seemed sorry, really sorry. And she should have been. But when Dawn said that, about choices? Oh man, with Grandma, something happened.

She put her hand on her heart and said, "I will live and die by the choices I make, Dawn Allerton. Thank you for that. Thank you."

She looked around at the crowd and there were plenty of people. Besides those who had come specifically to see the competition, more had sauntered up to see what all the commotion was about.

Grandma projected out, from her stomach, no doubt, "I have one thing to say."

Dawn Allerton had lost control like me.

"I want my family, my granddaughters Meg and Hattie, and all the good people of Jewel to know," Grandma said, "that what Ms. Allerton just said is true. You choose a path in life."

Oh my gosh. Was she doing a monologue? I sat in the dirt, right there where I belonged. She just made us lose. Was this the path she wanted in life?

She looked at me, and then she kept going. "You choose a path in life and that path can swerve, it will take you up hills and across meadows. It will take you over rivers and on top of rocks. It will take you to the highest summits."

I lay down on my side then and curled up. Diego sat next to me.

"And it will take you down to the lowest valleys."

She *was* doing a monologue.

"No matter where it takes us, we must not falter! We must be brave! We must"—she cleared her throat—"show the children!"

Then she started singing a song, I don't lie. She really, really did.

She started singing a song that was about children being the future or something.

She sang that, at the top of her lungs. And then Dad joined in, I swear to you he did—he was in the bleachers and he just started belting it out, he was singing with his mom about the beauty we kids possess inside. I rolled over on my face.

Soon Norma Knudsen was singing. Zoe's dad. My mom. All the adults in the crowd. Diego was giving me reports. "What is happening?" Diego asked.

I shook my face in the dirt, and some of it went up my nose.

At the very end of the song, I heard a voice joining in that I did not expect, a voice that was unexpectedly quite beautiful, with much vibrato. I turned to see if it was true, if it was really and truly true, and guess what, it was.

Dawn Allerton was singing with my grandma.

Dawn Allerton might be an opera singer.

And then it felt like the whole population of the lovely town of Jewel was also singing about the children of the world and their dignity, their dignity! on the hottest day on record, when Grandma had just blown the first challenge of the Strawberry Ambassador Competition after we had already almost been disqualified for flying away in a hot-air balloon.

This was my life.

Meg 1, Grandma 3

34

Reboot

No one spoke much on the way home, but there was a weird happy energy, probably from the group singing.

We had just lost in the worst turn of events ever.

When we got to the house, Mom said, "I'll help you take off the toilet paper, Meg."

"No thank you," I said.

I was not going to be accepting anyone's help at the moment.

Everyone sat outside talking about the competition and the music and the strawberries and the ha ha ha ha la la la, while I tore off toilet paper. They even called Grandpa Arthur on speakerphone to tell him about the day.

Did Grandma feel true remorse for what she'd done? Was this part of her war plan? Was she trying to make us lose?

I needed a reboot. I needed to restart. I needed to regain command.

The stuff that went down? Horrible.

My grandma? The worst.

Was I about to give up? No way.

When I was done de-toilet-papering, I went to my room, shut the door, and looked in the mirror we have on the wall.

"You can do this, Meg," I told myself. "You can rise from the ashes. She thinks she has the upper hand? She does *not* have the upper hand. You got this."

Someone knocked on the door.

"What?"

"Who are you talking to?" Hattie asked.

"No one," I said back. Then I whispered, "You can do it."

While Grandma was in the shower, I opened the next challenge in the privacy of the coat closet with a flashlight. I needed time to focus and figure out what to do myself first. Grandma would see the details soon enough, and I needed to plan.

FOOD TRUCK ROUND-UP
SPONSORED BY THE
JEWEL RESTAURANT ALLIANCE

The Jewel Restaurant Alliance is proud to be a part of the Strawberry Ambassador Competition. We proudly present a Food Truck Round-Up where contestants will use their creativity, ingenuity, and resilience to feed the good people of Jewel. The challenge is divided into three tasks.

Task 1: Using the strawberries you picked, you and your partner will team up with a food truck restaurateur to create a strawberry-themed delicacy. You will have limited time with the chef to discuss the recipe you would like to create. You then will have 2 hours to make the food.

Task 2: You will be provided with paint and other supplies to create a sign and decorate the outdoor dining area. Be sure to advertise both your charity and your culinary offering. This will need to be accomplished during your allotted 2 hours.

Task 3: You will sell your strawberry creation to the public at the Food Truck Round-Up beginning at 6:00 p.m. that evening. Food truck sales end at 9:00 p.m. You are allowed one helper in addition to

your team. All proceeds will go to your charity and will count toward your grand total for the finale.
Food supplies and paint/materials donated by the Jewel Restaurant Alliance and Hometown Crafts.

My heart pounded.

This was it.

This was the perfect challenge for me.

We were going to cook.

We were going to create strawberry-themed food.

I knew exactly what we were going to make and I knew exactly what food truck we needed in order to make it. I would have Hattie be our helper. Grandma doesn't even like to cook anymore except to make the most disgusting green protein shakes ever.

Finally.

Finally, a wave of true relief came over me.

This was my time to assert total and complete control.

35

Taffy Tussle

Guess what? Big news. Huge surprise. Grandma didn't agree with my strawberry food idea!

"I'm not sure that will sell the best," Grandma said.

We were sitting at the kitchen table and she had toilet paper wrapped around her hair again. "You know toilet paper doesn't belong on your head or your skin, right?"

"I say it does."

"You say toilet paper goes on bodies?"

"Absolutely," she said.

"What if there's another toilet paper shortage, Grandma?"

"That's an interesting question. If there's another toilet paper shortage, I will make sure to reuse and recycle."

Oh my gosh.

"It's a sacrifice for beauty." She fluttered her eyelashes. It was funny but I tried not to laugh.

"For real, though. Why do you do it?"

"Oh, it's to keep my hair nice when I sleep. I try to blow it out and curl it once a week. Otherwise it takes an hour to get it looking good."

I stared at her. Her hair was a big triangle.

"Do you want me to do your hair like this, too?" she asked. "We could be twins!"

"That's my dream come true, Grandma," I said.

"I knew it."

She really was one of my favorite people but right now she was the enemy and I needed to treat her as such.

"Let's get back to the task at hand. We have to get to the food trucks tomorrow at three. We want to be partners with My Fairy Treat Mother."

"Don't you mean your fairy godmother? And who is she?"

"No, My Fairy Treat Mother. It's Trudy Martin's food truck. She's our neighbor and she's a cooking genius." I took a breath and then I laid it all out on the table. "I'll be in charge of this challenge and we're going to make strawberry taffy."

Grandma scrunched up her face like she'd just been hit by a baseball or something.

"You want to make candy?"

"Yes, specifically taffy."

"Taffy?"

"Taffy."

That's when Grandma said, "I'm not sure that will sell the best."

"You've never had Trudy's taffy, Grandma. She makes the best in the state. Everyone knows about her and we can make different variations of strawberry taffy." I showed her my list.

Strawberry Cheesecake Taffy.

Strawberry Lemon Taffy.

Strawberry Shortcake Taffy.

Strawberry Salted Caramel Taffy.

"Salted Caramel?" Grandma asked.

"Yes. Strawberry Salted Caramel."

Then I had some more ideas and I scribbled them down right there at the kitchen table.

Strawberry Snickers Taffy.

Strawberry Mint Taffy.

"Meg. You're going too far."

"Too far?" I laughed. "You're telling *me* I'm going too far? Go bold or go old, right, Grandma?"

She ate a bite of cucumber. Mom, Dad, and Hattie had gone out for shakes. They'd wanted us to go too and I'd said, "Yes, Grandma, you should get a shake."

"Are you going?"

I shook my head. "No. I'm too tired." Really, I wanted to solidify my strategy, go over recipes, get everything in place without her hovering around. I was still simmering from the awful strawberry picking results.

"If you're not going, I'm not going," Grandma said.

"What?"

"We're partners. I'll stay here so we can get ready for tomorrow."

I looked at Dad, pleading with my heart and soul for him to save me.

He got the message. "Uh, Mom. Why don't you come along? I think you'll get a kick out of this ice cream shop."

"Nope. I'm staying with Meggy."

Sigh.

So here we were, in the kitchen, eating cucumbers and arguing over taffy, which we *would* be selling at the Food Truck Round-Up.

Strawberry sour cream.

Strawberry kiwi.

As I was coming up with ideas, Grandma abruptly stood up.

"Grandma. What're you doing?"

"I think we need to go bigger." She started opening cupboards. "Where does your dad keep my cookbook binder I lent him?"

"Grandma, we're making taffy. You don't need to worry about recipes or anything. I've got it."

She pulled up a chair and stood on it to look in the high

cupboards. I felt anger rising in my chest like water in a washing machine.

"I have it figured out, Grandmother."

"I know. I just want to look."

The cookbooks were in a drawer under the oven. The binder Grandma was talking about was definitely with them. I knew that, Grandma didn't.

"You mean that ratty old pink thing? I think he got rid of it," I said.

She looked at me. "Oh really?"

"Uh-huh." I kept my face very calm.

She opened the spice cupboard, the plates and cups cupboard. She looked under the sink.

"Why would he do that, I wonder," Grandma said. "Your dad loves to cook." She was getting closer to the oven. I stood up. "And he loves that binder."

This was true. My dad was into cooking and baking and brewing too. And Grandma gave him her recipes since she and Grandpa usually ate out now.

"Dad's been doing new things lately. He thought those recipes were getting outdated."

Grandma laughed. "Outdated?"

"Yes. Super outdated and old-fashioned." I walked over to the stove and stood in front of it, trying to look casual.

"I had a recipe for strawberry shortcake that was one of the most popular desserts at a church potluck one year."

"No one eats strawberry shortcake anymore, Grandma."

"Is that so? Your grandfather and I had strawberry shortcake at a buffet last week."

"Whoops. What I meant to say was no one under the age of sixty eats strawberry shortcake anymore."

Grandma gave me a side eye. "Nice one, Meg. Very nice."

Grandma looked on top of the fridge, in all the drawers, and in the pantry.

"I have a recipe for strawberry muffins from my Aunt Sue in that binder and a strawberry icebox cake but that would be hard to serve in big batches."

"We're making taffy."

She opened the dishwasher.

"You think we keep the cookbooks in the dishwasher?"

She smiled. "I think it's important to be thorough." She put a finger to her nose just like Dad and I do when we're thinking. "I think there might even be a strawberry rhubarb pie in there. Oh! We could do my freezer jam."

I folded my arms. I was not going to be let down. Not after everything that had happened the past two days. This was where I held the line.

"I'd like to look in the oven, if you could excuse me," Grandma said.

"We don't keep cookbooks in the oven either."

"You don't? Are you sure?"

"I'm positive." I was not moving. I was a boulder.

"Let me look."

"Nope."

"Why not?"

"They're not in there," I said, and though I was keeping my voice very steady, the sweat was starting to break out on my forehead. She was a bulldog.

"Maybe we should try on some costumes for the challenge tomorrow," I said. I was desperate.

"Oh, now you want to wear costumes?" Grandma asked.

"Uh, yes."

Grandma nodded. "Okay. Good. I was thinking you'd dress up as a Dalmatian and I'll be Cruella de Vil."

"That seems about right," I said. "After that dress trick you played on me in the strawberry fields."

"Well, I saw you had a copy of *Little Women* in your room and thought you should get a feel for how the girls lived," she said. "Also, you did steal my strawberry-picking clothes, so I had no choice."

She spotted the drawer I was guarding and then she looked at me. Our eyes locked.

"Grandma. Back away."

"I can't back away, Meg. I will not."

"Grandma. We're making taffy. It's been decided. Back away and go sing a show tune."

"You'd like that, wouldn't you?"

"I really would. I love your voice."

"I know you do," she said, and then, like a cheetah, she made for one side of the oven, but I was too quick and got in front of her, so she went for the other side and I blocked her. Then she did a dirty trick and went straight for my gut, tickling me like she used to when I was little.

"Hey," I laughed.

She lunged for the drawer and got it open.

Oh no. No no no.

"Not today, Grandma!" I yelled, and I dove and grabbed the beat-down pink binder, the pages almost falling out, right out of her hands.

"Meg! Let go. What are you doing!" But I was too fast. I got it and I ran.

I ran hard.

36

The Unplanned Attack

I ran through the kitchen and across the front room, jammed on my flip-flops, and bolted out the door.

Grandma was right behind me. "Get back here! Where do you think you're going? We need that!"

"No, we don't!" I yelled.

I ran down the driveway and onto the path to the lake. Grandma was in her nightgown with the toilet paper streaming from her hair. "Meg. Be reasonable." She had on Dad's tennis shoes and she was hobbling after me. "Just let me look."

But there was no way.

Grandma used to be an okay cook. Used to be.

She told us over and over again that she was done cooking, but now she needed that cookbook? She wanted to be the one who picked what we made? She was going to be in charge of a cooking challenge?

If I'd learned anything in the past two days it was that Grandma never ever gave up.

And from now on, neither did I.

I kept running down the path and I was getting tired and my lungs were burning.

Grandma kept following me.

"Go back home!" I yelled.

"No way!" she yelled back. "I want my recipes."

"This is war, Grandma. I'm not giving in and I'm not giving up."

"This is not war, Meg. This is grand larceny. I want my property back."

"They're Dad's."

"They're mine! On loan!"

I kept going. She'd run out of steam soon enough. I myself had a side ache of epic proportions, my body was sore from picking, and my feet were killing me. Don't run down rocky paths in flip-flops, it's not a good idea.

I ran until I got to the beach. It wasn't a big beach, there were trees and logs and my favorite humongous rock.

Grandma was nowhere in sight. She'd probably turned around.

I was relieved.

Finally, a victory.

I climbed up on the rock to catch my breath and lie down and maybe not die.

Why was she so stubborn? I had a completely reasonable and actually fantastic idea and she wouldn't listen. She always thought she knew best.

Sometimes I know best.

Sometimes kids know better than adults.

I sat up. And then I yelled, "I know best!" My voice echoed, bouncing off the water and the rocks. It felt awesome to hear it. Like someone was agreeing with me.

"I know way better than my Grandma Sally, who is out of control!" I yelled.

The echo yelled it back.

"Grandma Sally is not going to win!" I yelled even louder.

Oh, the sweet sound of my own voice.

Just then a bird swooped down and barely missed my head.

I screamed and almost fell.

"Watch it, bird!"

The bird flew up in the sky and looked like it was going to zoom back down. First the fox and now this?

"Leave me alone!" I yelled.

The bird flew back and forth overhead and I thought, what if she really did have some way to send animals to intimidate me? I wouldn't put it past her.

And then, as I was watching the bird get ready to

attack, Grandma was at my feet, reaching for the binder, which I'd set down.

"Stop!" I yelped and grabbed it and chucked it in the lake.

I couldn't believe I did it, but I did. I just threw it like a football.

We both watched as it sailed way way way out into the deep.

A big splash.

And then . . .

It sank.

The lake swallowed it up and everything went silent.

Like a dream.

And then she screamed. "NO!"

And she ran into the lake.

"Grandma!" I yelled. I scrambled to get down and ran in too.

Grandma dove and started kicking toward where I'd thrown the book.

Dad said Grandma was a terrible swimmer and she looked like a terrible swimmer and I didn't want her to drown and I thought she might drown.

"Grandma!" I yelled.

She was swimming sort of, but she was going nowhere, and she kept going under and then sloshing forward and then going under again.

"Grandma!"

I got to her and I pulled her back toward the shore. She

had wet toilet paper all over her and her green face mask was gone and she was furious.

"Unhand me!" she yelled as I dragged her.

"No," I said.

"Let me go right now."

My foot felt the mud and I said, "It's shallow here," and she started flailing and pushing away from me and so I let her go.

She stood up and fell back down and stood up again.

"Megan Amelia Stokes. I cannot believe you just did that. I can't. You had no right."

"Grandma, we're making taffy."

"I don't give a flying fig about taffy. Those were my recipes. Those were my mother's recipes. Her handwriting. My grandmother's handwriting. I let your dad borrow them under strict instructions to keep them safe. And you just, you you you . . ."

Her face was steaming mad and her fists were clenched, and I felt sick to my stomach.

"Grandma. I didn't mean . . ."

She cut me off. "No way. No way. I do not want to hear one more word out of you. NOT ONE WORD. You want a war, young lady? You got a war!"

And then she stormed into the trees.

Meg 2?, Grandma 3

37

Enemy Territory

I stood on the shore, my body trembling.

What had I done?

I had never seen Grandma so mad.

Ever.

I waded in and swam out into the lake.

I dove down but I couldn't see anything. I swam around and dove again and again.

I was about to give up when over in a tangle of branches and leaves, I saw a flash of pink.

The binder!

I swam as hard as I could, wiping away tears as I went. I got it!

I tried to swim back holding it over my head, but it was soaked and recipes were falling out of the page protectors.

I flipped over on my back and put the binder on my belly and kicked back to shore.

On the beach I assessed the damage.

Some of the recipes were lost causes. Others were blurry. Most weren't too bad. They were wet but just around the edges.

Why had I done it? Why?

I walked home, holding the binder like a baby.

When I got back to the house, Mom and Dad were standing on the front porch waiting for me.

I felt like a worm.

"Did you really throw the recipes in the lake?" Mom said.

I stopped in the driveway, my heart sinking into the dirt.

I couldn't talk. I really couldn't.

Dad took the binder from me and leafed through the pages, water pouring out of some of the plastic holders. He shook his head in disgust and set the binder on the railing.

"Garbage now," he said.

"No, it's not," I said.

"It is. It's ruined."

"It was an accident," I whispered, tears filling my eyes.

"An accident?"

I shook my head. "Not an accident. But kind of," I said. "She surprised me, and I threw it."

"Your Grandma Sally surprised you?"

I wiped more tears. "Yeah. I mean, she did."

I tried to explain. I tried to say how Grandma was being the worst and she wasn't listening, and she snuck up on me and I saved her. I saved her! I saved her from drowning!

"I am disappointed in you," Dad said. "These are family treasures you destroyed."

"Recipes are treasures?"

"Yes. Recipes are treasures. And you know they're important to me."

I swallowed hard. "Dad, they're all ripped and faded. You can barely read them."

"They were not yours to take, Meg," Dad said.

Mom sighed and sat down on the steps. "This competition was a bad idea. A bad, bad, bad idea."

"What? No, it wasn't."

"I think your mom is right, Meg. You two are at each other's throats."

My dad said that. My dad. The most competitive strawberry-loving guy I know. "Maybe we should stop this whole thing."

I shook my head. "No, Dad. No. She's, she's just, she, she's—" I couldn't think of the word. I couldn't think of what she was because she was so many things and I was so sad and mad and cold and embarrassed and soggy. "She's so hard."

Dad stared at me.

Then he said, "Meg, I don't think you realize what you've done."

"Dad. I'm sorry."

But he didn't care. He turned and went inside.

I sat next to Mom. "I made a mistake," I said. She pulled me close and I put my wet head on her shoulder. I was tired and sunburned and sore and awful.

"Do you think Dad's going to make us quit the competition?" I asked.

"Probably not," Mom said.

We sat like that for a long time. Daisy the cat watched me from the bushes; she was on Grandma's side too.

Mom stood up. "You coming in?"

I nodded.

Grandma was in the shower. She was not singing like she usually does.

I stood in the hallway and waited for her to come out.

Hattie was fake reading and stealing looks at me.

"Please stop," I said.

"What?" she said back.

"Don't look at me."

"I can't look at you?"

"No. You can't."

"We got you a shake."

"I don't want a shake and stop looking at me."

"Sheesh," she said.

But I was serious. I didn't want her to look at me. I didn't want anyone to look at me.

When Grandma came out, she walked right past me in a weird rainbow bathrobe and her hair in a towel and she went into my room.

"Grandma," I said, but she closed the door right in my face!

And on the door was a sign that said *STAY OUT OF ENEMY TERRITORY*.

Enemy territory? That was my room!

I knocked. "Grandma," I said. "I'm sorry. I'm so sorry."

She didn't answer.

I knocked again. "Grandma."

Nothing.

Hattie said, "Let me try."

"Grandma, can I come in?" she said. "It's me, Hattie."

The door opened a crack. "Grandma?" Hattie said.

Grandma said, "Only friendlies are allowed."

Then Hattie had to like squish inside the room through the barely open door! And Grandma slammed it once she was in!

I knocked again. "Hey! Can I come in?"

Nothing.

"Grandma? I at least need my pajamas."

The door opened a crack and my pajamas came flying out.

"And my . . ."

My pillow sailed out too.

And that was it. I was locked out of *my own room*. My own room declared enemy territory! I wondered how Dad would feel about that!

In fact, I went straight up to Dad's office, where he was writing.

"She kicked me out."

"She what?" he said, looking over the screen at me.

"I'm out," I said, plopping into the rocking chair. "She has taken over my room just like what happened to you."

Dad sighed. "I don't blame her."

"Dad! Don't you see? She's STOLEN MY ROOM!"

He looked at me. "Only the dead have seen the end of war."

I stared at him. "That's it? That's what you have to say?"

"I'm sorry, Megs. This is not my fight to fight. You took it to the next level. You escalated it."

I could've screamed. I mean really. I couldn't believe it.

He leaned back in his chair. "If you want to win this competition, you have to work with your grandma."

I closed my eyes. "I know, Dad, but now she's not even acknowledging my existence."

"I think she might need some time. I think *I* might need some time."

Was he that mad at me?

I slowly stood up. "Okay," I said.

"Okay," he said.

I went outside to sit by the binder, all beat down, wet and falling apart. Kind of like me.

"I'm sorry," I said to it.

"It's fine. I still love you," it said.

That didn't really happen but I wish it had. I wish someone had said that. I opened the binder and started pulling the recipes out of the plastic one by one and laid them out on the porch.

When I was done, I took them inside and carefully hung them on the drying rack in the laundry area with clothespins. By the time I was done, the entire rack was filled with old colorful index cards. It almost looked pretty. I wanted to tell Grandma what I was doing. I wanted her to come see.

But I knew she wouldn't. She was too mad at me.

I ended up sleeping on the uncomfortable couch in the front room that night. It's even worse than my wood floor, and I was surrounded by my grandma's costume boxes, which were all staring at me, mocking my pain.

How did this all go so bad so fast?

Just a few days ago, I had been happy, hopeful.

I was going to be in the Strawberry Days Ambassador competition and get Leaf bikes and drink lemonade all day long.

I stared at a brown spot on the ceiling where we'd had a leak during a rainstorm the summer before. I felt like that spot. I ruined everything.

38

Sea Witch

When I woke up the next morning, the house was nearly empty.

I walked into the kitchen and Hattie was eating cereal and listening to an audiobook.

Mom was at work. Dad was at work.

"Where's Grandma?"

Hattie took off her headphones. "What?"

"Grandma?"

"I don't know. She was gone in her truck when I woke up." My heart dropped to my stomach and I ran to our bedroom.

Her suitcases were still there.

I leaned against the wall in relief.

We had to be at the festival at three and I had no idea

where Grandma was or what she was thinking or what was going to happen but at least her CPAP machine was sitting on the bed.

I went to check on the recipes.

They were dry and stiff, but you could still read most of them.

My plan was working.

I carefully put each recipe in my old science binder I had from school that was in excellent condition. I typed up new copies of the recipes and put those in the binder too, in case someone had a hard time reading the originals. I also wrote up all the ruined recipes I could remember, starting with the Strawberry Pie.

Strawberry Pie

1 pie crust (could be graham cracker)

1 12-oz. package frozen strawberries (save juice!) or 1 ½ cups fresh berries

1 3-oz. package lemon Jell-O

1 pint vanilla ice cream

Thaw the strawberries and strain them for their juice. Combine the juice with water for 1 ¼ cups juice and water combined and bring to a boil on the stove. Add in the lemon Jell-O and mix until it dissolves. Mix in the ice cream and, once all melted, pour into a heatproof bowl. Leave to thicken for several hours. Add the strawberries and mix before pouring into the pie crust to cool and set. Serve with whipped cream.

Then I made a table of contents, an allergy warning, and an index for the back.

"What's that?" Hattie asked, coming into the office where I was working. I was drawing a portrait of Grandma for the cover.

"It's Grandma," I said, and held it up.

"That's pretty good," she said. "I think you got the shape of her hair perfect."

I smiled. "Thank you." I'd worked hard on that.

When it was all done, I put the binder on my bedside table so Grandma wouldn't miss it.

Then I waited.

While Hattie played with her ponies and listened to books and did regular summer things, I waited.

I waited outside by the driveway.

I waited in the front room looking out the window.

I waited on my bed, staring at the strawberry dream board.

I called her.

She didn't answer.

I called Lin.

She did answer, and I told her everything. She said it was understandable that I confiscated the recipe binder. "Strawberry shortcake would not cut it at this level of competition."

"Right?" I said.

"For sure." Then she said, "But that was pretty brutal to throw her recipes in the lake."

At lunchtime I made one of Grandma's gross green smoothies for lunch. Like eating her food might summon her home.

It didn't work.

I wrote down the recipe for taffy that I remembered from making it with Trudy.

I even put on the Ursula costume to see what I'd look like.

Hattie put on Ariel.

"These are awesome," she said as we both looked in the mirror. The seashells were way too big for Hattie, but the tail did look pretty good. The tentacles of my costume were ripped, just like my heart.

"She wouldn't just not show up, right?" I said to Hattie.

She looked at me in the mirror; the red wig made her look old and wise. "Did it actually sink?"

"I don't want to talk about it."

"Okay, but how far did it go? Past the beaver dam?"

"Way past."

"Whoa."

I was an evil sea witch.

An hour before we needed to leave, I was freaking out.

I called Dad. "She's not here and the challenge starts at three."

"There's still plenty of time, Meg. I'm sure she'll show up."

"What if she's quitting?"

"Grandma never quits anything."

That was true. She sure didn't quit bossing me around. "Maybe I should start walking," I said.

"It's up to you," Dad said. "It's pretty hot out there."

I looked outside. The trees. The dirt. The horses. Silent. Brown.

Every summer was like this.

I needed those Leaf bikes. No matter what had happened with Grandma, I needed them.

"I'm going," I said to Dad.

I hung up, then filled a backpack with water, snacks, and the taffy recipe. "Hattie," I said. "We're walking."

39

Grandma Sally Gets Serious

When we passed the horses and the haunted farmhouse, we heard it.

The rumbling of the monster truck.

We both stopped.

"Is it her?" Hattie asked. We looked down the street. We could see a dot approaching. A very loud dot.

As it got closer and closer, my heart grew bigger and bigger.

It was Grandma. Dad was right. She wasn't quitting. She was here with plenty of time before the challenge started.

She started honking about five feet from us and it was very loud and very unnecessary.

"Wow!" Hattie yelled, covering her ears.

Grandma stopped the truck on the side of the road

and for the first time in my life, I felt nervous to see her. I should have brought the binder.

When we climbed up and opened the door, music was blasting. BLASTING. It was so loud; I thought my eardrums might burst. "What are you doing, Grandma?!" I yelled.

And then I got a good look at her.

My Grandma Sally, in a complete chef outfit.

She had on a big old chef hat, a white jacket, checkered pants, red tennis shoes, and a name tag that said *SOUS SALLY*. Were there chef clothes in those costume boxes?

"Grandma, you look amazing!" Hattie yelled as we climbed in the back seat.

"Thank you!" Grandma yelled back.

"What were you doing all day?" I yelled.

She adjusted the volume to even louder, IGNORING ME, and pulled onto the road. Hattie and I looked at each other.

You try, I mouthed to Hattie.

She nodded.

"Grandma!" she shouted. "What have you been doing all day?"

"I can't hear you!" Grandma shouted back.

"What! Were! You! Doing! All! Day?!" I was actually pretty impressed with how loud Hattie could scream.

Grandma turned down the music.

"Well, Hattie, I had a great day. I went to the library and read up on war. Did you know I'm in a war, Hattie?"

Hattie nodded. "Uh, kind of."

"Oh yes. I am. And I have never been in a war before. My dad was in a war, as you'll remember, and he hated it. He hated war and thought it should be avoided at all costs. In fact, he was in two wars. One was much worse than the other." She glanced at me in the rearview mirror. "I also hate war very, very much, and my personal philosophy is things should be worked out, people should be compassionate and forgive each other. However, with war, one or both sides are not willing to cooperate, and that is how I ended up here."

I felt sick to my stomach.

"Grandma," I said. "I'm sorry."

She kept talking to Hattie.

"I'm not familiar with warfare so I felt like I should do some research." She held up *The Art of War*! And there was a stack of other books. "I went to the library and found some great resources. I also went to a place called Archibald's and picked an appropriate outfit for the competition today. I didn't want to rummage around at the house while you girls slept in."

That was where she got the cooking clothes. Lewis Archibald owned an antique and thrift shop and he had all kinds of things. Fancy plates, necklaces, wigs, blankets, books, statues, dolls, and apparently chef outfits.

"I love Archibald's," Hattie said.

I glared at her. She really did love Archibald's. Last year

for her birthday, she wanted to go there and look around—like that was her party. But love it or not, whose side was she on?

"Oh yes. It's a lovely place and I found wonderful treasures. I even got a uniform for you, Hattie, if you want to join me." She nodded to a plastic sack that was on the front seat.

I seethed! I seethed!

Hattie started bouncing in her seat! "Can I see it?"

"Let's wait until we get to the battlefield, oops! I mean the strawberry festival."

"Grandma," I said again.

She said, "Did you hear something, Hattie? I'm trying to be extra vigilant and watch out for any attacks from the enemy."

Hattie looked at me. "Uhh, I mean, Meg just said something."

"Who?"

"Meg. Your grandkid?"

"Oh yes. That's whom the war is with, did you know? My own progeny, blood of my blood, daughter of my son. Can you imagine?"

I was destroyed. Defeated. Sunk. She checked out my war book? She got a chef outfit for both her and Hattie but not me? She was ignoring me? That was the worst of all. I was her *enemy* enemy?

The new binder I had made now seemed silly. Grandma was never going to forgive me.

I put my forehead on the glass and watched the fields go by.

Meg 2, Grandma 4

40

Deep-Dish Trouble

When we got to the park, the festival was in full force. The carnival was set up with a Ferris wheel, a roller coaster, a Tilt-A-Whirl, a ride that shoots you straight up in the air. Bounce houses, a foam pit, blow-up sumo wrestling. There were carnival games and horse rides and a dunking booth. And then all kinds of stands were set up with people selling things. Lin and her brother were selling friendship bracelets and jewelry. I usually help with their booth and it's one of my favorite things because Lin and I would use the money to buy cotton candy and play Skee-Ball.

This year I had bigger things on my plate. The war with Grandma and those Leaf bikes, which were up on the main stage again, glistening in the sun.

"Where do we go?" Grandma asked.

"Over there." By the big pavilion parking lot there was an area sectioned off with five food trucks lined up: My Fairy Treat Mother, Arlene Pizza's Parlor, Stan's Burgers, Doughnut Dugout, and Super Sliders.

I sat up. Eyes on the prize, eyes on the prize.

"Grandma, listen, we want My Fairy Treat Mother," I said as we pulled in. "I know you think I'm a bad person and you learned about war strategies and you're mad and all that, but this is serious. We must get My Fairy Treat Mother. We must. If we don't get My Fairy Treat Mother, we go for Stan's Burgers. If we don't get that, we do Doughnut Dugout or Super Sliders. We do not, I repeat, WE DO NOT want Arlene Pizza's Parlor."

"That's true, Grandma," Hattie said. "Arlene Pizza's Parlor is the worst restaurant ever."

I stared at the back of Grandma's head and pleaded. I pleaded. Arlene Pizza's Parlor was practically out of business it was so unpopular.

Grandma put the truck in park.

"First of all, Meg. I don't think you're a bad person. Just a misguided one. Second of all, what's wrong with Arlene Pizza's Parlor?"

I shouldn't have said anything. I SHOULD NOT HAVE SAID ANYTHING. The worst thing you can do in war is show your weakness. But then again, what was I supposed to do? I had to warn her.

"Grandma, please. It used to be run by Arlene Pizza, this awesome lady who is an amazing chef and her last name really is Pizza so it is kind of perfect. She is the best but now she retired and moved to California and her son Jesse runs it and he makes the worst pizza ever."

"The worst?"

"The worst. He's trying to be high-end. Like he has a pizza with seaweed on it."

"Dried seaweed? Or pickled?" Grandma asked.

"I don't know what kind, Grandma. Does it matter?"

She shrugged. "I like seaweed. It sounds like he has a vision."

No.

NO!

"Grandma. It's not good. He puts fried eggs on pizzas. He has one with lentils. There's one with, with—" What else. What else. I looked at Hattie. "Tell her some of the other bad ones."

"Dad said there's one with bone marrow," Hattie said.

"Bone marrow, Grandma! On a pizza! That's disgusting. How did he get the marrow, Grandma? How? How?" I was really beating it in.

"Dad said it wasn't too bad," Hattie said. "Lots of people actually like that one." I shot her a look.

"Grandma. I'm serious. This is important. We cannot pick Arlene Pizza's Parlor."

She sat thinking.

Please, please, please.

Then she said, "I wonder what a lentil pizza would taste like? I used to make lentils for the kids all the time."

My heart stopped. Curse the lentil example.

"Grandma," I said. "Listen."

She turned and looked at me. "No, you listen. You threw out the old, you think old is bad, so I'll do what you want. In with the new, my girl."

And with that she opened the monster truck door, jumped down, and walked straight for Jesse of Arlene Pizza's Parlor, chef clothes and all.

"Whoa," Hattie said.

"I'm in deep trouble," I said.

"Deep-dish trouble!" Hattie cackled.

41

Betrayal

I followed Grandma out of the truck, which was no easy feat because I had to get past Hattie, who was trying to put on her new chef outfit, get over the seat, open the five-thousand-pound door, and then jump ten feet.

Nevertheless, I persisted.

I jumped out of the truck and ran across the parking lot to the food trucks, where Grandma was already in conversation with Jesse Pizza, who had his hair in two French braids that looked pretty dang cool, I have to say, and was also wearing a full chef outfit and large combat boots.

"Grandma," I said, out of breath. "We need to go stand by the other participants."

"Howdy," Jesse said.

I gave him a nod before trying to get Grandma back on track. "We're supposed to be over there," I whispered.

Everyone was gathered around Dawn Allerton, who was of course looking at us with disdain in her eyes. I guess the group vocal performance about the children yesterday didn't soften her. "Care to join us, Group Stokes?" she called.

Grandma shook Jesse's hand and said, "I am so pleased to meet you, one creative to another."

"I'm pleased to meet you," Jesse said. Grandma had a habit of buddying up to everyone except the one person we needed to be friends with. Dawn Allerton.

We walked over. "Please, trust me, Grandma."

"What if he's actually really good, Meg? What if he's the best and you just don't know it yet? I would have made a great Miss Hannigan but they didn't give me a chance."

"Grandma, he's not."

She shook her head. "This might not be a battle you want to pick," she said.

"I do want to pick this battle, Grandma. You can have all the other battles," I said, which was not true. I was giving up zero battles, but I was desperate.

Hattie walked up wearing an oversized white jacket and checkered pants.

"Ah, look at that!" Grandma said. "It's perfect."

"I love it," Hattie said. She wouldn't look at me, which was just great.

Dawn Allerton started talking. "Okay, people, first of

all, let's review where each team stands and the money that has been raised so far."

Ugh.

"We have Zoe and Mark in the lead with twelve hundred and fifty dollars."

We all clapped. Zoe smiled and her dad bowed. I took some deep breaths and thought about dogs in the ocean again.

"Next we have Meg and Sally Stokes at a thousand dollars."

Grandma waved. I just stood, hands behind my back crossing my fingers, hoping that the reminder of our tragic downfall yesterday all due to GRANDMA would soften her heart and for once, she might listen to me. Just say no to Jesse Pizza.

Someone, I think it was Dan, yelled, "Great outfit, Mrs. Stokes!"

"Yes," Dawn Allerton said. "Team Stokes is getting quite the reputation for their choice of competition wear."

"Thank you!" Grandma said. "And thank Lewis Archibald of Archibald Thrift!"

Everyone clapped. Sigh.

"Then we have Diego and Dan Martinez with seven hundred and fifty dollars."

"WOOT!" Diego yelled, and gave Dan a high five.

"Then Rich Bailey and Cooper Hedengren in fourth at five hundred dollars."

Mr. Bailey raised Cooper's hand and then spun him in a quick circle as if they were part of a dancing competition, and I do like those two, I have to say.

"And then last, but not least," Dawn said, but they did have the least, "we have Ellie and Tamara Hansen with three hundred and fifty dollars. Let's give everyone a round of applause." We all clapped again. It was a little anticlimactic.

Dawn then told about all the food trucks and their long history in Jewel and how they were carefully selected because they were hometown favorites that got their start in the community.

"Except Arlene's no favorite," Diego whispered.

"Hasn't been since Jesse took over," I whispered back.

"They're just trying to be nice by having him. Whoever gets that truck is going to lose hardcore. One time my dad brought home a squid pizza from there."

"Squid?"

"Squid. I didn't take a bite and I never will," Diego said. "That place is the worst."

He was right. Diego was right. He knew because he was from here. Everyone from Jewel knew, Arlene Pizza's Parlor was not a food truck you wanted to get tangled with.

"I am going to pick your team name out of a hat and you then get to choose which food truck you'd like to work with for this competition," Dawn said.

I waved to Trudy Martin, who winked at me, which

was exactly the right thing to do. Better to not let everyone know that we were going to be partners.

"Okay, first we have . . ." Dawn put her hand in a black bag. *Be us, be us, be us.* "Sally and Meg Stokes."

I yelped! Hooray! A miracle!

"We'd like to work with Arlene Pizza's Parlor," Grandma said as quickly as she could.

My jaw dropped.

I tried to grab the microphone, but it was too late. Dawn had pulled out another partnership.

Diego and Dan.

I watched in horror as Diego said, "We pick My Fairy Treat Mother."

I looked at Grandma.

She patted my shoulder.

"War hurts."

Meg 2, Grandma 5

42

Strawberry Fight

We walked over to the pizza truck and I had a rock in my chest. I was so mad at Grandma.

So so so mad.

"Jesse!" Grandma said. "This is exciting."

"I love your energy," Jesse said. "I never dreamed I'd get picked first."

No one else dreamed you'd go first either, Jesse Pizza, I wanted to say.

"Of course, we were going to pick you. I feel like we're kindred spirits," Grandma said.

Jesse Pizza beamed. I did not beam. I did the opposite of beaming. Hattie took a step closer to me and I forgave her for her Archibald chef clothes. I needed her as an ally.

"You're right. I think we are kindred spirits," Jesse said. "Let me guess, you gravitate toward artichokes."

"I love them." She looked at me, smiling. Grandma had taught us how to cook artichokes and dip them in mayonnaise and ketchup when we were kids.

"I knew it," Jesse said. "I'm a food reader on top of being a pizza artist. I can tell a person's favorite fare just by looking at them."

A food reader? A pizza artist? This guy was the worst.

He pointed at Hattie. "Potato chips."

Hattie gaped. "Yes! I love potato chips."

That was easy. All ten-year-olds love potato chips.

"Salt and vinegar?"

Hattie grabbed my arm. "How did you know?" she said.

That was a lucky guess.

He looked at me. "Hmmm," he said. "You're a little harder."

Yes. Yes, I was. I folded my arms.

He closed his eyes and raised his arms and held them up there for like a thousand years.

"Isn't this exciting?" Grandma whispered.

"Shouldn't we be starting on our food?" I said back.

"Shhh," Grandma said. "Don't break his focus."

We stood there. Finally, he opened his eyes, "Jalapeño poppers."

"Nope." I looked at Grandma and Hattie with a smirk.

"Hate them. Can't stand them." And that was the truth. They used to be my favorite. USED TO BE. But then one time me and Lin ate like a hundred of those things at her cousin's wedding and we both were sick for days. Now I can't look at them without feeling queasy.

"Hmmm," he said. "There's something blocking your food waves."

"Yes," I said. "My food waves are blocked."

That was because my food waves were at the My Fairy Treat Mother food truck. That was where they were, and Jesse Pizza and my grandma were going to take me down unless I came up with something.

"Would you like to enter my laboratory?" Jesse said, gesturing to the truck, which used to be painted with giant pepperoni pizzas on the side but now was painted boring white with a black stripe.

"Absolutely," Grandma said.

"Yes," Hattie said.

"Fine," I said.

It was tight in there.

He had a huge pizza oven that took half the truck, a small sink, a counter for dough, and then a wall of ingredients with little labels. Hanging from the ceiling were all kinds of plants.

"These are my babies," he said, lovingly touching the pots. "They're from my garden back home." He started naming them like they really were his children. "Basil," he said, touching a leaf. "He's so sensitive. I mean, he loves so much but he also can get his feelings hurt in an instant."

No. Just no.

"Oregano, oh my goodness. She's such a hard worker," he said.

"I feel that about oregano too," Grandma said. UGH.

"And here we have sage, rosemary, dandelion. The three of them together can be a force of nature, though they have been known to get out of hand if I let them."

What did that even mean? I looked at Grandma and of course she was eating this up.

"Nasturtiums." He pointed to some flowers.

Nasturiwhat?

"Pansies and bachelor buttons. These flower buddies are my powerhouses. I try to put them on as many pizzas as I can."

That was it.

"Uh, can we come up with a plan? We don't have much time," I interrupted.

They all looked at me, surprised. Like somehow the weird flowers in this place had hypnotized them and they were happy to spend all our allotted time meeting the plants.

"You put flowers on pizza?" Hattie asked.

"Absolutely. I put beauty on pizza," Jesse said. "My mom thinks I'm being too out there. She always made, you know, regular old pizza. And that's her style. That's her thing. But I'm different. People don't want pepperoni anymore. They don't want barbecue chicken or Hawaiian," he said. "They want innovation. They want flavor explosions. They want, well, love."

Grandma put her hand to her chest. "Wow," she said. She was entranced by Jesse Pizza. I was not.

"How have things been going, financially speaking?" I asked, because I knew that people in Jewel wanted pepperoni. They wanted barbecue chicken. They would pay good money for a Hawaiian pizza. We were humble traditional folks or whatever. Not fancy-pants weirdos.

Jesse looked sideways at me. "Financially speaking?"

"Yeah. You know, money," I said.

"No one cares about money," Grandma said, who had once upon a time told me taffy would be bad for sales.

"Yes, they do," I said. "Money is how we win."

"Meg," Grandma said, but Jesse Pizza put up his hand.

"It's okay, Sally. She's right. I've been struggling." He touched his nasturti-whatever flowers. "Mom had a great business and a huge following and since I took over, you know, it's not the same." He looked at Grandma. "I keep thinking do I give the people what they're used to, or do I give them what their soul is calling for?"

"You give them what their soul is calling for, that's what you do," Grandma said. "You are a brave pioneer."

Jesse was wrong. Grandma was wrong. However, there was no time or need for this fight.

"Luckily," I said, interrupting, "we don't have to worry about all that right now—we just have to focus on today, and today we are not making pizza. We are making taffy."

Grandma looked at me. "You're still on taffy?"

I was on taffy. I was on taffy until death.

"Yes," I said.

"But won't Trudy Martin make taffy?" Hattie asked.

"I don't know. Maybe Diego and Dan will make something else. I feel like taffy is the right choice for us."

Jesse folded his arms. "You remind me of me."

Oh brother. I was NOT like Jesse Pizza in any way. At all.

"A firecracker," he said. "Stubborn, driven, afraid."

Afraid???

Then he said, "We can't make taffy. We don't have burners in here."

"What?"

"There's not a stovetop. I just have a pizza oven and I left my hot plate at home."

I looked around. He couldn't be serious. No stovetop? Nowhere to boil anything?

"This is a pizza truck, not a taffy truck, my sister."

I looked at him in disbelief.

We really did have to make pizza. All my plans were ruined.

"Don't worry," he said. "I will create the masterpiece pizza you never knew you wanted."

43

Grilled Spam Strawberry Pizza

One of the rules of the Food Truck Round-Up was you had to work with whatever ingredients were in the truck you chose plus the crates of strawberries you picked yesterday. Along with the flowers and plants, Jesse Pizza had weird stuff. Weird, weird stuff.

Jesse and Grandma started talking about ideas—at the moment they were discussing Grilled Spam Strawberry Pizza. "I think it's the texture that could really make it, Sally. You're going to love it."

We were not doing that. I had to figure out what we were doing, though. I let them think they were getting somewhere while I devised a plan.

I gave Hattie my notebook that I keep in my pocket. "Write everything down. We need to think."

"Okay," she said.

I started listing off the labels on the ingredients.

Polenta	Fresno Chiles
Spinach	Black Beans
Meyer Lemon	Pico de Gallo
Tomatoes	Pork Belly
Fried Capers	Peppers

"Don't touch those. They're ghost peppers, they'll burn your mouth out," Jesse Pizza said when he saw me inspecting them.

Farm Eggs	Peanut Butter
Honey Nut Squash	Heavy Cream
Cotechino Sausage	Onion Creme
Spam	Mascarpone
Thai Peanut Sauce	Mozzarella
Chicken	Kiwis
Spring Onion	Pineapple
Spam	Brussels Sprouts
Ramen	Salami
Fennel Sausage	Guanciale

What was Guanciale? I didn't know what half these things were.

Asparagus

Marshmallows

Why did he have so many marshmallows?

"Why do you have so many marshmallows?" I asked.

Jesse Pizza looked at me, his face red. "Those are for personal use." He looked at Grandma. "They give me energy."

Jesse Pizza liked to eat marshmallows while he made pizza. He had bags and bags of them stuffed in a cupboard.

He went back to talking fungi pizza and I had the most brilliant idea I have ever had. Not really. But a pretty good one.

"Why does your face look like that?" Hattie said.

I have an idea.

"Grandma. Jesse. I have an idea." They looked over at me.

"What?" Grandma said.

"Dessert pizza! Dessert pizza! Dessert pizza!" I kept saying it. I'm sorry but I couldn't stop. "It's so obvious. We could make the best dessert pizza. It will be so good. We can make a strawberry sauce and put marshmallows on top—you have so many marshmallows—they could be the mozzarella cheese of our strawberry pizza. We could also use the kiwis and pineapple. Everyone will love it!"

Grandma looked intrigued!

Hattie said, "Yes!"

Jesse flared his nostrils. "Sorry, my friends, I do not do dessert pizzas."

"What? Why?" I asked.

"It's just, I don't believe in them," he said, putting his hand on the pizza oven.

"What are you talking about?" I said. "We have to do it."

Grandma looked at Jesse and then back at me. She was still in her full chef stuff, jacket and hat and all, and it was hotter than lava in here.

"I think we should hear Meg out, Jesse."

She said that! She knew it was a good idea! Victory!

"Nope," he said. "I can't. I can't do it."

"You can do it," I said.

"No. That's what they'd expect us to do."

He started pacing and it was way too small a space for that. He had to get past Hattie first. "Excuse me," he said. "Dessert pizza is not my brand. Excuse me." He got by Grandma. "And I don't think, you know, excuse me"—now past me and turning back around—"competing with other dessert trucks, trying to make dessert when that's not our expertise, excuse me"—past Grandma again—"is a good idea. Excuse me." He went past Hattie and now he was by the pizza oven.

He stopped, thank goodness. "I built this oven by hand. My mom used a standard pizza oven. This is my baby and it was meant to make my kind of pies. Not kitschy dessert pizzas."

Grandma folded her arms. "He has a point. I once ate a cinnamon roll pizza at the worst pizza restaurant I had ever been to. It was truly unappetizing."

"See! I won't do it. I won't. They won't cook properly anyway," Jesse said.

"Grandma," I said. "No one is going to eat Spam strawberry pizza around here."

"Oh, I think they might," she said. "They'll be curious."

"Yes, exactly," Jesse said. "Exactly my vibe. And I have other strawberry ideas too. I have millions of strawberry ideas."

"Grandma," I said. "I'm sorry, Jesse, but we'll lose. Hattie. Tell her to listen," I said.

Hattie looked scared.

"I don't like Spam," she said, which was kind of helpful but not all the way helpful.

Grandma took off her chef hat and rubbed her forehead. Was she breaking?

"How about this," she said to me. "You and Hattie go set up outside. Jesse and I will come up with three pizzas that we think could be hits. We'll all try them and then make a decision."

"We don't have time for that," I said.

"We'll be quick about it, right, Jesse?"

"Sure. Pizzas are fast."

"That's right. Pizzas are fast, and we have to set up outside anyway, sis. Just give him a chance."

"I'd really appreciate a chance, Meg," Jesse Pizza said.

Oh my gosh.

"Grandma," I pleaded.

"End of discussion, Meg. Let him do his thing."

Meg 2, Grandma 6

44

Dis-included

Hattie and I were thus kicked out, banned, dis-included.

"I can't believe this," I said to Hattie.

"I'm sorry," Hattie said.

We had a small part of the parking lot designated as Arlene Pizza's Parlor dining space. There were three picnic tables off to the side, a garbage can, a table with Parmesan cheese and pickled carrots, which was weird, and water, plus a potted tree.

"Why is there a tree?" Hattie asked.

"I don't know."

We looked at the other trucks and they all had potted trees too. No one was out decorating because they were all inside working AS A TEAM on their food. The worst part was, Grandma should be decorating, not me. She was the one who had learned how to upcycle. She was the one who plastered her room with dream boards. She was the one who was driving around in a monster truck with stripes. She had flair.

I, on the other hand, cooked dinner almost every night either with my dad or with Hattie. I made cookies and cakes and pies on the weekend and once I made up my own pudding out of melted chocolate. I should be in that truck.

We moved the picnic tables out to the middle of our dining area.

Then we stood there.

"I think we're done," I said to Hattie.

"Should we, like, decorate or something?"

I shrugged.

"Grandma!" I yelled. "Did you have any kind of vision for this place?" She opened the food window.

"What?" She'd put on a hairnet. "What did you say?"

"What should we do out here?"

"Catch," she said, and threw me the keys to her truck. "You can find some stuff in the back and definitely decorate that tree. We don't have a lot of vertical space."

"Grandma, you're the one who knows how to do this."

"Oh puffo! Get going," she called, and then shut the window.

I sighed.

"I thought we emptied the truck," Hattie said.

"If Grandma says there's stuff, there's probably stuff," I said.

And yes. There was a lot.

First of all, there were some griddles from the pancake breakfast that Dad hadn't taken back to work. There was the bag of Aunt Jenny's weird dolls. There were still a few boxes of costumes. A box of props. An old door. A couple dress forms. A box of sheets and blankets. Another box with masquerade masks, feather boas, sunglasses, some fake food, and a giant plastic foot.

Oh, and my tuxedo hat and jacket, which I'd chucked in there with rage when I'd gotten back from the balloon fiasco.

Dawn Allerton told us we could use whatever we had on hand, plus any of the poster board and other supplies she and her assistant had brought.

We had a lot of stuff.

Most of the teams would probably use the Dawn supplies, so was this an advantage? All the junk Grandma had?

Except I had no idea what to do with it.

I groaned. "Help me pick up the door."

Hattie and I lifted the door and it was heavy and I was trying to get it over the back of the truck and I yelled, "Do you have it?" and she said, "No, I don't have it," and then I was flattened by the stupid door.

"Are you bleeding?"

I was lying on the asphalt with the door on top of me.

"Probably," I said.

"This is the worst," Hattie said.

We tried to make the picnic tables look nice. We put the dolls in the middle for centerpieces and we cut out cardboard pizza slices and scattered them all over the ground.

We leaned the door up against the end of the food truck.

"What's that for?" Ellie called. She was stringing lights to her tree, which looked very elegant, and where did she get lights?

"It's to welcome people to our truck!" I yelled.

"With an old door?" she said.

Diego was putting up lights too. Did they all think to bring lights? Was there some fancy light memo I missed? "What are you guys going for? Junkyard?" he asked.

"We're going for eclectic!" I yelled back. "Mind your own business."

We both looked at the mess we'd made.

"It's hopeless," I said.

Hattie nodded. "It *is* kind of bad." Then she said, "Maybe we could make it a photo booth."

I looked at Hattie. "That is the most genius idea!"

"Thank you," she laughed.

I hugged her. It's not that a photo booth was going to make us win, but people like those things and it was so smart.

We got one of the sheets and draped it over the door.

"Get the masks and boas," I said. Hattie ran. "And the fake foot!"

We set up a bunch of props and costumes for people to use. We put the foot by the door and then hung the tuxedo jacket and hat on the dress form. We made a sign that said *TEAM STOKES WISHES YOU THE BERRY BEST NIGHT! ALL PROCEEDS GO TO THE ALZHEIMER'S ASSOCIATION.* Then we pinned it up.

It looked amazing. We did something amazing!

Grandma opened the window. "Girls," she said.

We looked over.

There was flour on her face and green sauce on her apron.

"Come try our pizza."

45

A Victory

Grandma and Jesse made three kinds of pizza. Strawberry Blue Cheese Onion Creme Pizza. Strawberry Thai Peanut Nasturtium Pizza. And last but not least, Strawberry Fennel Sausage Pizza with Fried Parsley and Funghi Misti Mushrooms.

We stared at them.

"What are they called again?" Hattie asked.

Jesse said the names of the pizzas again.

"They are ah-mazing!" he cried.

Grandma folded her arms; she seemed rattled. Hattie looked at me. This was the first time we'd seen Grandma seem off her game and to be honest, it was unsettling. Maybe Grandma had met her match with Jesse.

"They look pretty good," I said.

The pizzas were cut in tiny slices. Grandma said, "I hope you like them. We're trying to decide which one to feature."

Hattie took a bite of the strawberry fennel one.

Hattie started coughing.

Hattie almost died.

"What's wrong?" I said. She was hacking now; I hit her back and Grandma got her a glass of water.

"Is it bad?" Jesse Pizza said, crestfallen.

Hattie's face was bright red. "It's hot. It's so, so hot."

She gulped down the water.

"Oh," he said. "I did use a spicier sausage on that one."

Jesse took a bite of the pizza, closing his eyes as he chewed. "It's subtle. She must be sensitive."

"I told you we should ease off on the hot sausage," Grandma said.

"Sally, I have to go with my gut."

She sighed. "Try the pizzas, Meg."

So I did.

The strawberry blue cheese one was strange, but the flavors worked surprisingly well together, I must say.

The Thai strawberry peanut one took a few bites to get used to. The nasturtiums were kind of peppery. It did have a slight peanut-butter-and-strawberry-jam undertone, but I kind of liked it.

"This one's good," I said.

"I've been thinking about that one, Jesse. What about allergies?" Grandma said.

It was true, no one was allowed to bring anything with peanuts to school. That could limit our customers.

"Oh, allergies," Jesse sighed.

And last but not least, the one that almost killed Hattie, the weird sausage mushroom one. Though not for everyone, it was by far my favorite—sorry, Hattie.

"Can I get the recipe?"

"Of course," Jesse said.

I was surprised but I really did like his pizzas.

"They're good, Jesse."

"Thank you," he said, beaming.

"Normal people around here don't," Hattie said. She was sitting at a picnic table, recovering.

"Are you serious?" Jesse asked.

I felt kind of bad for him. I knew what it was like to have your ideas shot down.

Grandma sat next to Hattie. "I'm sorry, Jesse. I think she's right."

Jesse ate another piece of the mushroom one. "How can anyone not love this?"

"You don't think it's going to work?" I asked Grandma.

"I don't," she said. "You were right about the dessert pizza."

"I was right?"

She nodded. "You were absolutely right."

She looked at Jesse. "I think we need to do it, Jesse. Even if it hurts your soul. I'm so sorry."

He shook his head. "Really?"

"Really," Grandma said.

He looked at me. "Fine. This is wrong, but fine."

I clutched my chest. "Be still, my heart!" I said, and Grandma laughed.

"You have to tell everyone it was your idea. I had nothing to do with it," Jesse told us.

"We will!" I said. "We'll take all the credit."

I looked at my watch. We had under an hour left.

Grandma stood up. "Jesse and I will finish up out here. You and Hattie figure out your pizzas." She put her hand on my shoulder. "This time *I* should have trusted *you*."

Hooray! The tide was turning!

Meg 3, Grandma 6

46

The Beginning

Hattie and I got to work. She rolled out the crusts. I made strawberry glaze and put on the marshmallows.

We'd never baked in a pizza oven and it took us a few pizzas to get it right but we did!

"Grandma!" I yelled out the window. "I think we figured it out."

She and Jesse were tying a purple ribbon into the tree. She came hurrying over.

"Show me."

She took a bite.

She looked at Jesse. "You have to try this."

He walked over. "What do you call it?"

"Uh, it's Strawberry Marshmallow Surprise."

"Great surprise," he said, sarcastically, which was rude.

"Try it," Grandma said.

He took a bite. He looked at me. "What's on this? This isn't just marshmallows."

"It's the surprise. I used some mascarpone. I thought it might go well with the sweet."

He smiled. "It does. Smart girl."

I laughed! It was good! He liked it!

Maybe we could really win.

We got all the ingredients ready because we wanted to make the pizzas fresh for our customers. "Fresh is really the only way," Jesse said.

We made a couple of variations, like a kiwi strawberry glaze and a pineapple glaze with strawberries on top. I even let Jesse put a strawberry nasturtium pizza on the menu. While we were working on all that, Hattie went on a spy mission and found out the following things:

- Ellie and her mom were making strawberry smoothies. They looked pretty good and they even had a green smoothie. Grandma said she was going to buy one. I said no way. She said, "Meg. I'm buying one. Maybe I'll get ideas."

- Zoe and her dad were making strawberry sliders. They were having issues with texture.

- Cooper and Mr. Bailey made strawberry shakes. Hattie said it smelled like brownies, though, so there could be some kind of brownie strawberry shake combo, which was a very smart idea.

- Ellie and Tamara Hansen were making strawberry doughnuts—delicious! Tough competition, but they were in last place, so I wasn't too worried.

- And Diego and Dan were making taffy. So many kinds of strawberry taffy. I tried not to care. Hattie nudged me. "I guess Grandma was right about that one. We would have been in trouble if we tried to compete with them."

I nodded. "I guess."

"Ten minutes!" Dawn Allerton yelled.

"Ten minutes?" Grandma cried.

"We're ready," Jesse said. "Don't panic." And it was true. We had pizza dough balls ready to be rolled out. We had gallons of strawberry sauce prepared. We had marshmallows and mascarpone divided in containers.

Dawn Allerton and Keoni came around to each truck. "Don't forget, people, competitors must wear a strawberry mask at all times so no one knows who is selling what food. We want this to be anonymous. A true test of your skills."

"What?" Grandma said. It was the first time I'd heard her object to doing something weird.

"You have to be in disguise, Ms. Stokes," Dawn Allerton said.

She handed them to Grandma, giant strawberry-shaped masks.

"You really expect us to wear these all night? It's a hundred degrees in here."

"No pain, no gain, Ms. Stokes. Also, and you'll enjoy this one, if you choose to leave the truck for the bathroom or to take a break in our participant tent, you must put on a strawberry poncho along with the mask to disguise your identity." She handed us three gigantic strawberry-decorated plastic ponchos.

"Really?" Grandma laughed.

"It's not funny," Dawn Allerton said.

"It's kind of funny."

"Shh, Grandma," I hissed. Dawn turned and went to the next truck.

"Do you they think these ponchos will confuse people? When they see Dan in one and me in one, they won't be able to guess who is who?"

She had a point. "Who cares," I said. "Just put it on."

"Oh, I will. Don't want to break Allerton's rules."

We all put on our masks.

Jesse Pizza started giggling.

"Do we look good?" Grandma asked.

"You look good," he said. "So good."

And we went back to pizza preparation.

It was happening! We were making dessert pizza! It was delicious! Grandma and I weren't fighting! Jesse Pizza was actually a good pizza artist! Everything was how it was supposed to be.

At the stroke of six, Dawn clanged a gigantic gong signaling the start of the food truck round-up.

The crowd was huge. Bigger than the balloon festival.

People were already lining up and taking pictures at our photo booth.

This was going to be the best night.

Dawn got on the microphone. "Welcome, to the Strawberry Ambassador Competition Food Truck Round-Up. All proceeds from your purchases tonight will go to the various charities you see advertised here tonight and will help these young future leaders advance in the competition."

Everyone clapped.

"We hope you will be generous and open with your wallets and your hearts. Have a fabulous evening, and let the eating commence!" Dawn said.

Everyone cheered.

Then the pizza oven broke.

47

Broken Dreams

It broke.

It stopped working.

There were no flames inside the oven.

None.

It broke.

"Jesse!" I said. "What do we do? What do we do?"

Jesse said, "Don't worry. This happens all the time."

He tried to fire it up again. Nothing.

He tried again. Nothing.

A third time. No.

"Can you just light it manually?" I asked, sweat pouring down my strawberry face. "Like throw a match in there?"

"Uh, no," he said, looking at me like I was crazy. "Don't worry. I got this."

Meanwhile, there was a line at our truck across the

parking lot and clear to the grass. Hattie and Grandma were taking orders.

"Strawberry Marshmallow Surprise!"

"Kiwi Pineapple!"

"Chocolate Supreme!" That was a new one I made up at the last minute, and it was pretty good.

I gave Grandma slices from the experiment pizzas we'd already made, my hands shaking.

Soon we ran out. No more pizzas. Nothing.

"Another Strawberry Marshmallow Surprise!" Grandma yelled.

"Jesse," I said. "Can you fix it? Please fix it. Can you fix it?"

"I don't know," he said. "It's worse than usual."

Worse than usual?

Worse than usual?

My whole life flashed before my eyes.

"Kiwi Pineapple!" Hattie called.

He looked at me. "Maybe I should've gotten it looked at before this."

WHAT??????????????

I staggered over to Grandma and Hattie. "Hey," I whispered, between shouts of orders they were taking. There was a crowd gathering waiting for their pizza by the picnic tables. "Psst," I hissed. Grandma looked at me. "The oven is broken. Stop the orders."

"What?"

269

"The oven," I said, nodding toward Jesse. I could barely breathe.

"The oven is broken?" Hattie said so loud that people at the window heard.

"The pizza oven is broken!" someone yelled.

"No pizza here!" someone else yelled.

"Wait! No!" I shouted. "We're fixing it."

Jesse was pulling it apart. Screws and metal and all kinds of pieces lay on the floor of the truck.

Me, Grandma, and Hattie looked at each other in strawberry masks.

"We're doomed," Hattie said.

I felt dizzy. *What did we do?*

I waited for Grandma to tell us how to save this.

She grasped my hand. "What do you think, Meg?"

"What?"

"What should we do?"

She was asking me.

Me.

I swallowed hard.

People were starting to leave. I couldn't let her down. I couldn't let our team down. I couldn't let Great Grandpa Jack down.

"Grandma, will you distract the customers? Keep them entertained? I'll figure it out."

She nodded. "Of course I will. You can do this, Meg. I know you can."

"Go Meg," Hattie said.

My heart swelled. This was it. This is what a true strawberry champion did. This is what all the preparation was for. A true strawberry champion was resilient. They worked hard. They rose to the occasion. I knew it. Hattie knew it. Grandma knew it. This was my moment.

I threw on the strawberry poncho and ran out of the food truck.

I wove through the crowd looking for Dawn Allerton. There were so many people. Some would step aside for the frenzied strawberry, others had to be told.

I couldn't find her.

"Dawn Allerton!" I yelled. "Dawn Allerton?"

I ran to Grandma's monster truck and climbed up on the back. "Dawn Allerton!" I screamed.

Then I saw her. She was eating a doughnut and holding a bag of taffy! Was that fair?

Whatever. I ran to her. "Dawn. It's me."

"Don't reveal yourself."

"Oh my gosh. Fine. I'm the strawberry selling pizza," I said.

She took a bite of doughnut. It looked delicious. "Proceed," she said.

"Well, Jesse Pizza's pizza oven is broken, so we can't cook our pizza."

"Is that a tongue twister?" she laughed.

"No! I'm not joking. It's broken! You have to do something. We can't make our food!"

She considered this. "It's completely broken?"

"Yes!" I cried. "Please!" I cried. "Can we join with another truck, can we use someone else's oven? What can we do?"

She studied me for a minute, considering.

Then she said, "I'm really sorry about this, but I don't think it would be fair to let you join another team. You picked the truck; you get whatever comes with it." She handed me a taffy and walked away.

48

Last Ditch

She walked away. I stood there in disbelief. She just walked away.

So I ran.

I ran back to the truck.

I got out a griddle from the back.

I ran it to our dining area. The crowd was getting smaller, but Grandma was out in a strawberry poncho and mask standing on a table singing.

She really was.

She was singing "Easy Street" from *Annie,* and she was good. People were laughing and taking video and pictures.

"Is that a Broadway star or something?" someone asked. "Who is that?"

I have to admit, my grandma was pretty rad even if she

was out of control and my sworn enemy and got me into this whole mess in the first place.

I ran to the other picnic table and set down the griddle. I saw Dad in the crowd. He was smiling at his mom and singing along. He knew who we were, of course. There was no disguising Miss Hannigan.

I ran to the food truck, sweating like crazy. "Jesse! Do you have an extension cord?"

"What?"

"An extension cord?"

He sat on the floor still trying to fix the dumb oven. Hattie was telling people that pizzas were going to be ready in no time and please don't leave and if they wanted, they could enjoy the singing strawberry.

"Why do you need an extension cord?"

"DO YOU HAVE ONE?!" I yelled. Jesse froze. I inspired true terror in him, which was what I was trying to do. This was an emergency. Then he said, "Uh, yeah."

"Sorry," I said.

"It's okay," he said. "I understand. Maybe your food is passion fruit."

"It probably is," I said.

He found an extension cord.

"Bring the pizzas that were ready to cook and all the ingredients and everything outside, both of you," I said. I know I was bossing everyone, but a lot was on the line. I was going to save this challenge no matter what.

I ran out with the extension cord and plugged in the griddle.

Then I got another griddle from the truck.

"Where's the pizza?" someone yelled.

"Coming!" I yelled back as I ran through the crowd, griddle over my head.

When I got back, Jesse and Hattie were standing at the table each holding a pizza. Grandma was now singing a song about a matchmaker.

"You're going to cook them on the griddle?" Jesse asked.

"Yeah," I said.

"That won't work," he said.

"It will work."

He shook his head and I didn't care. I didn't care. It was going to work.

I plugged in both griddles, turned them on, and waited for them to heat up while surveying the damage.

Diego's truck had tons of people. All of the trucks had hundreds of people, including ours, but they were leaving us. They were leaving! I had to fix this!!!

I put the first pizza on.

Hattie and Jesse stood there watching. "It's the toppings that will be the issue," Jesse said.

And it was true. The bottom of the crust cooked but the marshmallows on top didn't melt a bit.

I had to do my best. I had to. Maybe a raw marshmallow on a burned crust with strawberry sauce would taste good?

I handed a slice to a lady who was waiting.

"Here you go, ma'am," I said, breathing in my own hot breath in the mask.

"Is it supposed to look like this?" she asked. We both looked at it.

"Yes," I said. "That's our signature pizza look."

She looked over her glasses at me. "And you can cook it on a griddle? That's okay?"

"It's great."

She took a bite.

I grimaced as she did it, but she couldn't see my face.

"It's not bad," she said to her boyfriend or friend or whatever they were.

Be still, my heart! Be. Still. My. Heart!

She took another bite and then covered her mouth.

In disgust? In love?

"What's wrong, babe?" the guy said.

She spit it on the asphalt.

I gasped. I mean, was that necessary? She had to spit it? The line of people that had formed behind her were all witnesses to her expectorate—that means spit.

"It's raw," she said. "I want my money back."

Oh no. Oh no no no.

"Maybe take another bite."

"No way," she said.

"I'll do it," her boyfriend said.

That did not go well.

"Money back," he said.

Everyone wanted their money back.

"Just wait!" I cried.

A man said, "This is very unprofessional."

Someone else said, "Waste of time."

Another said, "Dessert pizzas aren't good anyway."

I looked at Jesse to see if he wanted to gloat.

"I liked them, Meg," he said. "I really did."

Hattie and Jesse started giving people back their money.

I looked at Grandma, who was still on the table singing. She was singing even though there was hardly anyone left in the area.

She was not giving up. I was not giving up. I was not!

I put another pizza on the griddle. "This one is going to be delicious!" I yelled to nobody.

It was not delicious.

I tried something else. I smashed some pizza dough with a few marshmallows and a handful of strawberries and made a kind of marshmallow flatbread and cooked it on the grill. I convinced a group of kids to buy it.

No one else would even look at it.

"Please! It's delicious!" I yelled.

Nothing.

I sold an old couple some strawberry stuffed marshmallows that I made that weren't too bad. I think they felt sorry for me.

Grandma stopped singing.

She stopped.

And the silence was deafening. I mean, it wasn't silent. There were hundreds of people laughing and talking and enjoying all the other food trucks. But when Grandma stopped singing, it meant something.

She and Hattie and Jesse sat at the picnic tables. Two strawberries and a chef.

I kept going, tears blurring my eyes. I made strawberry dog biscuits. People had dogs. They needed to feed their dogs. Dog biscuits. Dog biscuits!

"Strawberry Doggie Food!" I yelled. "Strawberry Doggie Food!"

"Flour isn't great for dogs," Jesse said.

I kept yelling. "Strawberry Doggie Food!"

No dog lovers lined up. Not one.

I finally sold them to Lin.

"Jesse says they aren't great for dogs," I told her, when I was bagging up all twenty I had made.

"Oh, these aren't for my dog," she said, popping one in her mouth like a true second in command and best friend.

And then it was all over.

The entire dining area, photo booth and all, was empty.

They went to buy doughnuts and taffy and burgers and shakes.

Hattie took off her strawberry disguise and I thought

Dawn would come get mad, but no one cared what we did. We were nobodies. We were failures.

I tried to breathe. *Breathe, Meg. Breathe. You can fix this. You can figure this out. You can do this.*

And then I really started to cry.

I pulled off my dumb mask and wiped my stupid face and I cried. I cried and cried.

Grandma walked over.

"Hey, sister." She put her arms around me. "Hey. Hey there." And she hugged me, one strawberry to another.

Grandma didn't let go. She held me.

"Is the war over?" she asked.

"I think everything is over," I whispered.

Meg 0, Grandma 0

49

White Flag

At home, I lay on my bed in the dark.

Someone knocked on the door.

I rolled over and pulled the pillow over my head.

"Meg?" It was Mom.

"Please leave me alone," I whispered.

"Meg?" she said again. She didn't hear me.

"Please leave me alone," I said again.

She paused for a minute and then I heard her walk away.

I thought maybe I would climb out the window. It was late at night. Everything was dark but I knew if I went out the window and ran, I could get to the lake, I could get in a canoe, I could row away. Maybe the fox and the bird would come along. Maybe I belonged out there with them.

There was another knock. This time louder. "Meg. Let me in." It was Grandma.

"It's okay, Grandma," I said.

"Please, Meg?"

I closed my eyes. I'd been rude to Grandma. I'd yelled at pretty much everyone. I'd sold my friend doggie treats. I was in last place in the Strawberry Ambassador Competition.

"Please?" Grandma said.

"I'm fine," I said.

"I have something for you," she said. "It's important."

"Okay," I said.

Grandma came in and she had the toilet paper in her hair and green stuff on her face.

"Hey," she said.

"Hey."

She sat next to me.

"I brought you some green algae cream for your face and some toilet paper for your hair." She held up a toilet paper roll.

Oh my gosh.

"No thanks," I said.

"Sit up," she said.

"Grandma. I'm not putting toilet paper in my hair. I'm done with toilet paper."

"I think you should do it," she said.

I lay there, feeling miserable. I couldn't believe how badly everything had gone.

"Come on, goose," she said. "This will help."

"Okay," I whispered.

She wrapped the toilet paper around my head.

When she was done, she put a big old green glob of cream on my face.

"What is this anyway?" I asked. It was cold and tingly and smelled like mint.

"It's your best friend right now. Say 'hello, best friend.' "

"What?"

"Say it, say 'hello, best friend. Thank you for being nice to my face.' "

"You want me to say that?"

"Of course, I do."

"Hello, best friend. Thank you for being nice to my face," I said. It did feel good, Grandma putting it on my skin. My nose, my chin, my cheeks, under my eyes where tears started to leak out.

"Hey now," she said. "You don't want to cry the healing mask away."

I laughed.

"You can't laugh either!" she said. "You'll crack it."

"Okay," I said, the stuff drying and tightening around my mouth.

When she was done, Grandma said, "Now lie back and relax."

I did what she said and lay back on the pillow. Grandma wiped her hands and lay next to me.

"Do you feel better?"

I shrugged. "I guess." I looked at her. "Does this stuff make you feel better?"

"Usually it does," she said. "It helps me pay attention to what I'm feeling at the moment. Not something I felt earlier. Not something I think I'll feel tomorrow. Something I feel right this minute."

I thought about that.

"So, what's the verdict? How does it feel right this minute?" she asked.

"Cold," I said.

"Yes."

"And smelly."

She laughed. "I like how it smells."

"Yeah," I said. "Me too, kind of."

She looked over at the bedside table and sat up. "What do we have here?"

I looked at what she was holding. I'd forgotten about the binder of recipes.

"It's nothing," I said.

"Did you do this?" she asked, looking at the drawing on the cover.

"Yeah," I said, embarrassed.

"It's so good," she said. "I think you got me."

"Not really," I said. "It's dumb."

"This is not dumb," Grandma said. She started to leaf through it while I stared at the ceiling, trying to feel right now. "Be still, my heart." She laughed.

"What's so funny?" I asked, sitting up.

She was looking at a recipe for meatloaf.

"I'd forgotten about this one. I had to make it for dinner one night when my mom was working late. I put it in and went to watch my Dracula show and almost burned down the entire house."

"You did?"

She nodded. "I was grounded for a week."

"You were grounded? You like Dracula?"

"Uh, yes and yes. I love Dracula. And Frankenstein and all the good monster shows."

I had no idea.

She turned the page.

"Oh, I love that one," I said. It was a recipe for chocolate chip chocolate cake that me and my dad made a few times.

"That's the best recipe in here," she said. She looked at me. "Have you ever had it with canned pears?"

"No."

"You have to have it with canned pears and frozen raspberries. I should have written that in for your dad."

"I can retype the recipe," I said. "I've typed them all up in case people can't read them."

"You did?"

I showed her new ones.

"Wow," she said.

I smiled.

She looked at every single recipe, laughing and making

comments. When she was done, she looked at me. "This means so much to me."

"I ruined it."

"No. You didn't. You made it better."

She put her hand on mine. "I'm sorry I got so mad about this," she said. "Even though I'm thrilled you've re-done the binder and I'm happy to have it back, I hope you know you're a million times more important to me than these recipes."

My lip started quivering.

"I'm sorry I threw it," I said, tears coming for the mil-lionth time. "I can't believe I did that."

Grandma sighed. "I had it coming."

"No, you didn't."

"Yes. I think I did."

We sat in silence for a bit.

Then I decided to say it, say all of it.

"What I mean is, I'm sorry for everything. I'm sorry I've been mean. I'm sorry I didn't trust you. I'm sorry I'm a bad partner." I took a breath. "I just, I wanted those bikes so badly and I thought I knew how to get them." I looked at her. "I wanted them so much that I didn't, you know, I didn't care about your feelings and I made you go to war when you didn't want to."

"Oh puffo," she said. "I'm going to tell you something, and I need you to listen."

"Okay," I said.

She took a deep breath. Then she said, "I was embarrassed when I didn't get that Miss Hannigan part. I thought, you know, no one needs me anymore."

"What are you talking about? Of course people need you."

"No, they don't. Not really. Your dad and Aunt Jenny grew up and are doing great and living their lives. Grandpa is busy with work." She sighed. "I've been lonely."

"You have?"

I never thought my grandma would be lonely. She seemed like the least lonely person on earth, actually.

"Pretty darn lonely. Maybe how you feel out here in the summers. Like you can't get anywhere. Like you're alone."

I nodded. "Yeah," I said.

"I've been wanting to be a part of something. I had my heart set on that play and when that didn't work out, I felt hurt. Then your dad told me what was going on with you." She paused. And then she said, "I know you didn't want me to come. I know that I wasn't your first choice. I know I can be difficult."

"Grandma."

"Let me finish." She clasped her hands together. "I know I can be difficult, and I can be stubborn. My dad used to say I was single-minded. Peter is like me in that way."

"Me too," I said.

"I'm going to agree with you on that." She winked at me.

Then she said, "I know you would've rather been with your dad, but Meggy, this has been the most fun I've had in years. *Years*."

"Really?"

"I loved every part of it. I loved that we went in a hot-air balloon together."

"I actually loved that too," I said.

"I knew it!" she said, smiling. "I also loved sleeping in the bed with you and talking at night. The look on your face when I said I was moving into your room, oh my land, priceless."

"Grandma!"

"I'm serious. I could have gone to a motel and I know it would have been more comfortable but I couldn't bear it. I really couldn't. I wanted to be here."

I nodded. "It was more fun."

"It was incredibly fun. I even love that you threw my clothes in the shed! That was hilarious! It reminded me so much of the war with Grandpa Jack when Peter set his alarm clock in the middle of the night."

"I still can't find my boots."

She laughed. "I can't find my overalls and I need those for the *Oklahoma!* auditions."

"We'll find them."

"We better," she said. "It's a plum part."

"Of course it is," I said.

She smiled. "I also love that we got to pick strawberries and I could show you how I do it. I could show you that I'm actually good for something."

"Grandma, I know you're good for something."

"I know you know that, but sometimes I don't know it." She stopped talking and looked at the window.

"I feel like that sometimes too," I said.

She looked at me. "Do you?"

I nodded. "Yes," I whispered. "Kind of a lot."

Grandma hugged me again. "We are good for something, right? Whether we win or lose, or get the part, we're good for something. We're good for something just because we are, right?"

"Yes," I whispered.

She went on. "And well, we've raised money for my dad, my dad who I miss so much, and that means a lot to me." Now she was crying.

"I'm sorry, Grandma," I said. I couldn't imagine not having my dad here. "I wish I could have met him."

"Oh, me too, sis. Me too."

I could have sat there forever, Grandma hugging me, my face cracking with green algae, toilet paper wrapped around my head. I was happier than I had been in a long time.

Then her phone beeped.

She took it out of her pocket and looked at it.

"They just posted the standings in the competition. Do you want to know?"

I didn't really want to know. But also, I did.

"Okay," I said.

She looked. "You were right about your Fairy Treat Mother friend. Diego and Dan pulled ahead. They have three thousand, three hundred and forty-five dollars."

"What? Over three thousand? That's so much money."

She laughed. "It really is. Zoe and her dad have three thousand and five dollars. Cooper and his uncle have two thousand and sixty dollars. Ellie and her mom have one thousand, six hundred and nine dollars."

I couldn't believe it. "They sold that much food?"

"It was the biggest crowd in the history of Strawberry Days, I guess."

I flopped back on my pillow, dislodging the toilet paper I bet. "And we made like ten bucks."

"We made more than ten bucks. We sold a few pizzas and some people felt bad for us and donated money anyway. We have one thousand, five hundred and forty dollars."

"We do?"

"Yup."

"That many people gave us money last night?"

"Yes, they did. People pay for a heartfelt effort," Grandma said. "Whether the result is delicious or not."

"Maybe they were paying for Miss Hannigan's performance."

"Good point," Grandma said.

It was kind of a lot of money but also not near three thousand. "I wish we had raised more."

"We have a heck of lot more than we had three days ago," Grandma said.

"That's true."

I looked at her. I looked at her green face with wrinkles and lines and somewhere under all the goop, an age spot. "Do you want to keep going?"

She touched her toilet paper hair. "I mean, I don't think the people have seen enough of us yet, do you?"

I laughed. "No. I don't think they have."

50

To Grandpa Jack

Grandma and I went out to the front room.

Mom, Dad, and Hattie were all talking on the couch.

"We're not giving up," I said.

Right when the words came out of my mouth, I felt a burst of energy. We were not giving up.

Mom looked at Dad. Hattie said, "Really? You can't win."

Grandma put her hands on her hips. "Hattie, do you quit when the finish line is in sight? Do you stop when the odds are against you? Do you throw in the towel just because you're losing?"

"I sometimes do," Mom said, and laughed.

"Me too," Dad said, nudging Mom. "But you're right. You shouldn't." He glanced at me. "You're up for this?"

"Yes," I said. "We want to get more money for Grandpa Jack." I looked at Grandma. "We can do it."

"Of course, we can."

Over root beer and popcorn, we read the final challenge. It was almost midnight.

THE FINAL CHALLENGE

RADLEAF RELAY

Presented by Silvio Radleaf

You are in for the time of your life! In this final challenge, you and your partner will be participating in the first ever Radleaf Relay. Meet at the stage promptly at 10:00 a.m.* Each part of the relay will be explained, and at 10:30 a.m. the race will begin. We anticipate big crowds.

*Matching uniforms/T-shirts/athletic wear is encouraged.

"To Grandpa Jack," Grandma said.

"To Grandpa Jack," I said.

We all clinked our root beer glasses.

51

The Final Challenge

At ten a.m. on the dot, Grandma and I were standing on the stage at Kiwanis Park, in the clown jumpsuits. It was the only thing matching we could find, and they were surprisingly comfortable. Grandma had gotten up early and finished jumpsuits for Dad, Mom, and Hattie too, so we were all dressed the same. It was both the worst and the best. My dad's jumpsuit was a little snug and none of us could stop laughing.

"I knew you'd love them," Grandma said.

"*Love* is a strong word, Grandma," I said.

Our goal was to make as much money as we could for Grandpa Jack. That was it. The bikes were a distant dream at this point.

"Hey, Meg," Diego said. He and Dan were in tank tops and basketball shorts.

"Hey," I said. "Congratulations on being in first place."

"Thanks. I'm excited."

"You should ride your bike to Prince Edward Island."

"What?" he said. "Where's that?"

I sighed. "Never mind."

We both looked at the Leaf bikes. "Maybe you can borrow them sometime and go there."

"Maybe I will," I laughed. If only he knew what kind of epic trip he was offering.

Once everyone was seated on the stage, Dawn Allerton got the microphone. There were hundreds of people at the festival and a lot of them were at the stage to see how the final challenge would go down.

"We are pleased to have so many of you join us in the Radleaf Relay, the final event in the First Annual Strawberry Ambassador Competition!"

Everyone cheered.

I saw kids from school. I saw Mom and Dad and Lin and her family sitting together. I saw my teachers. I saw Trudy and Jesse Pizza and Mr. Biddulph.

"Look over there," Grandma said, pointing to the parking lot.

It was Grandpa Arthur and Aunt Jenny! They just pulled up!

"What?! How did they get here?" I was so happy to see them.

"I called them last night right after the food truck and told them to jump in the car and come see our final challenge."

I couldn't believe it. "You didn't even know if we were going to *do* the final challenge!"

"Oh puffo. We were always going to do it. I knew you wouldn't quit. And I wouldn't dream of having your grandpa or Jenny miss it."

Dawn Allerton's voice broke in. "So far we have raised over ten thousand dollars for the charities that these young people have chosen!"

More cheers.

"And today, after the Radleaf Relay, which is not for the faint of heart, I have to say, one lucky pair will be the proud owners of these two beautiful Leaf Electric bikes!"

Keoni threw confetti on the bikes, which was weird but kind of cool.

Everyone was screaming.

I took a deep breath.

"I'm sorry, goose," Grandma whispered.

"It's okay," I said, wiping a tear away, which was dumb, but it was there.

"And now to explain the relay that he designed, we invite a former resident of Jewel, Mr. Silvio Radleaf!"

He was here?

The cheers were even louder as a man in a full bike

outfit, like the tight shorts and fancy sunglasses and a shirt that said *Leaf Bikes* and everything came up on the stage. He looked bigger than on his TED Talk.

I sat up straighter.

"Hello, Jewel!"

Everyone went wild.

Grandma grabbed my hand.

"Are we ready for this?!" he yelled into the microphone.

More cheering.

He looked at us and smiled. "Well, I have some big news. It is my pleasure not only to announce the various events in this relay but also to say that the winner of to-day's relay will receive five thousand dollars from the Rad-leaf Company for their charity!"

My heart.

I looked at Grandma. Five thousand dollars?

"Grandpa Jack," she said.

"Grandpa Jack," I said.

"Second place will get four thousand and on down to one thousand for the team that comes in last."

"Not us," Grandma said.

"Not us," I said back.

"Here's what's going down," he said. "Today we have an innovation relay. To begin, all of the competitors will line up at the starting line at the far end of the east soc-cer field." We all looked over; someone had painted a big yellow strip across the grass clear down at the other end of the park. "Each partnership, at the signal, will race to the Leaf bikes waiting for them at the other end of the field."

Diego gave Dan a high five.

It was true, Diego was the fastest in our grade and I'm sure Dan was pretty fast himself.

"The catch is," Silvio said, "teams will be using stilts to cross the field."

I yelped!

This was a miracle!

It was a Strawberry Days miracle!

Grandpa and my family were hugging each other and bouncing in their seats!

Radleaf went on. "Stilts were known to be utilized clear back in ancient Greece and used throughout history not only for entertainment but for practical uses such as getting through marshy land, crossing rivers, and climbing over fences. People had a problem; they came up with a solution." I had no idea. "Today we'll use them to slow some of you down."

People laughed. I did not. I was too excited. I'd been practicing on stilts for months and Grandma was even better than me!

"Once you cross the field, you will ride your Leaf bikes over to the carnival grounds, where you will both enjoy a turn on the iconic Tilt-A-Whirl—which was invented in 1926 by Herbert Sellner in his Minnesota backyard. His backyard, ladies and gentlemen! It doesn't take much to make something amazing! It's been used at carnivals and fairgrounds ever since. The Tilt-A-Whirl goes every three minutes so if you don't get on in time, you'll have to wait for the next round."

"I've never been on a Tilt-A-Whirl," I whispered to Grandma.

She looked at me, shocked. "What? Are you serious?"

"I'm afraid of getting sick. I don't even like merry-go-rounds. Remember what happened with the roller coaster?"

Grandma thought a second. Then she said, "You know what, you'll be fine."

I nodded.

Walk on the stilts. Ride the bikes. Get on the Tilt-A-Whirl.

"Next you'll hop back on the Leaf bikes and ride to the food truck area." I knew where that was all too well. "Each partnership will be given a large vat of strawberry Jell-O with plenty of whipped cream on top. One competitor will hold the Jell-O and the other, with their hands behind their back, will eat their way to the single strawberry hidden in the bottom of the pan."

"No hands?" Grandma said.

"You have to use your face," I said.

"For Pete's sake."

"Jell-O was eaten clear back in Victorian times but was trademarked in 1897 when May and Pearle Bixby Wait mixed strawberry, orange, raspberry, and lemon flavoring with gelatin and sugar to make Jell-O in their kitchen. A couple put their heads together and came up with one of the most iconic desserts of the century."

I really did love Jell-O.

"After you've found the strawberry, get on your bikes and ride back to this area. Once you get to where Keoni is standing"—he pointed to the back of the crowd, and I realized that there was a big sheet of plastic stretching in the middle of the seats from Keoni to right in front of the stage where we were sitting. I thought it was for keeping people from filling in too much—"you will Slip 'N Slide all the way to the stage and hit this bell." A guy brought out a huge bell.

"Slip 'N Slide?" Grandma whispered. "Is he kidding?"

"The Slip 'N Slide was invented by Robert D. Carrier, an upholsterer who made the coverings for seats in boats. When he came home one day and found his son and his friends with the hose, sliding down his painted concrete driveway on their bellies, he had an idea. He brought some slippery fabric home and put on the water and watched the entire neighborhood have the time of their lives."

Grandma sighed.

"I wanted to sponsor this competition because I believe in you kids! I believe in crazy ideas and intuitive invention!

I believe in seeing problems and finding solutions! I believe in hard work and partnership! And I believe in all of these people up here!"

Clapping! Cheering! Laughing!

I loved Silvio Radleaf. I think Grandma did too because she was squeezing my hand very very hard.

"And today is the day, my friends! Today is when we celebrate young people and the bright future, full of new things, new stilts, new Tilt-A-Whirls, new Jell-O, new Slip 'N Slides, and new electric bikes!"

Even more clapping!

People were standing up!

My dad looked like he was going to burst—in a floral jumpsuit!

Silvio Radleaf turned and gave us all high fives, which was a little awkward, but I loved it anyway. I yelled, "Thank you, Mr. Radleaf!" Diego laughed but I didn't care.

Silvio Radleaf then took his seat and things got serious.

Dawn Allerton got on the microphone. "Okay, people, okay. Let's keep things down." She warned all the spectators to stay out of our way. "We have roped off sections for observers, please be courteous." And then she led us off the stage.

"We're doing this, Grandma."

"We are, my girl. We really are."

52

Be Still, My Heart

"Please get on your stilts," Dawn Allerton said into the microphone.

I helped Grandma onto hers. She helped me onto mine. We stood together.

Diego said, "How do you do this?"

Dan fell over.

Everyone was falling over. Grandma and I stood. Waiting for the signal to start.

People were lined up along the entire soccer field and we were right by the side where Grandpa and Jenny and Mom and Dad and Hattie and everyone else was. "You can do this," Dad yelled.

"Go hard!" Hattie yelled.

"Think about dogs running in the ocean!" Jenny yelled.

"I'm nervous," I said to Grandma.

"Oh, sis, it's a piece of cake and you know it," Grandma said.

I nodded. A piece of cake. We could do this.

"Stilters," Dawn said. "On your mark. Get set. GO!"

Diego started walking fast and fell on his face.

Dan fell on top of him.

Mr. Bailey surged and also fell.

Zoe too.

"Slow and steady," Grandma said, as we walked.

And we did go slow.

And steady.

Grandpa Arthur was walking along the sideline in his dress shirt and bow tie saying, "Focus, focus."

Dad was saying, "Go faster! Mom, go faster! You guys can go faster than that!"

Grandpa said, "Stop distracting them."

And Mom yelled, "Ignore them! Just keep going!" and we did.

When we got to the end of the field, the others were way behind us.

"And we have Team Stokes in the lead," Dawn Allerton said over the PA. "Team Stokes, in their colorful, uh, body outfits, are now getting on Leaf bikes."

I looked back. Diego and Dan were catching up.

"Hurry, Grandma."

"How do you do this thing?" she asked.

"You just pedal and push the power button."

I got on and started riding.

"Meg!" Grandma yelled.

I turned around. She was straddling the bike, studying the handlebars.

"What button?" she yelled.

Now Dan was at the bikes. And Diego wasn't far behind.

"Grandma!" I said. "Just go. Just go."

She looked at me. "I will not go. Come back and help me."

Oh my gosh. I rode back. "This button, Grandma. If you pedal, and then push that, the motor will start. You can make it go as high as you want, the engine will help you go."

Diego rode by us! Dan too!

Grandma saw them. "Oh puffo," she said. She got on. "Let's go!" she said.

She started pedaling and then clearly pushed the button because soon she was zooming ahead. "Wait!" I yelled, and I got on mine.

We reached the Tilt-A-Whirl as Diego and Dan were getting in their car and the operator was about to close the gate. "We're coming!" I cried, and we barely got on.

"That's not fair," Diego said.

"They made it," the operator said.

"We did make it, Diego," I said, trying to catch my breath. We rode those bikes fast.

Zoe and her dad and Ellie and were pulling up but it was too late. They'd have to do the ride after us. I could see Cooper and Mr. Bailey getting on their bikes back at the soccer field. People were lining the path all the way from the soccer field cheering us.

"All right everyone, buckle up," said the operator said.

I sat next to Grandma, who was sweating and fanning her face. "Those bikes are amazing. I must have been going twenty-five miles an hour. I want one."

I laughed. "That's the whole point, Grandma!"

I looked over at Diego and Dan, who were pointing at the gate and whispering. We had to run as fast as we could to the bikes once the ride was over. "Grandma," I said, "see the back exit? That's where we go."

"Okay." Then she said, "Diego and Dan. You two really hustled. Good job."

Oh my gosh.

"Thanks, Mrs. Stokes," they said.

"There's Grandpa," I said. He and Dad and Lin were red-faced and pushing through the crowd. Mom and Jenny and Hattie weren't far behind.

The operator started checking all our seatbelts and my stomach plummeted.

Grandma turned to me. "Now listen up. Close your eyes."

"Close my eyes?"

"Close them. And say to yourself, 'This is going to be fun. I'm not going to get dizzy. This is no problem.'"

"Are you sure?"

"Close them. Think good thoughts."

"Here we go," the operator said. I closed my eyes and there was a whirring sound and soon we were moving. Slowly at first and then faster and faster. Music blared over the speakers and now we were spinning and jerking.

"Oh no!" I screamed. My stomach lurched. "Is it supposed to do this?!"

"You're fine!" Grandma yelled.

"No, I'm not!"

"Yes, you are!"

I opened my eyes. The world was blurring and our bodies were being thrown around and there was Dad's red shirt and now there was a girl in a pink dress and now a lady with a big hat, and Dad again. Grandpa.

"Grandma! I'm going to throw up . . ." But then the ride slowed down and I tried to breathe. Breathe.

"You're okay," Grandma said. "You're okay."

"I'm okay."

"You're okay."

"I'm okay." The ride stopped.

I stood up. I covered my mouth and it almost happened. Almost.

"Keep it together, Meggy!" Grandma said.

"Go without me," I gasped.

"No way."

I stumbled toward the back gate. Grandma put her arm around me. "Meg."

"Go without me," I said again. "I'll catch up." My belly was bubbling and I couldn't see straight. Why would anyone go on those things?

"I'm not going to leave you," Grandma said. "Just think mind over matter. Think, 'I'm okay.'"

"I'm okay, I'm okay," I said.

Dad and Lin were cheering. The other competitors were on the Tilt-A-Whirl now. I saw Silvio Radleaf in the crowd. I could do this.

Then I realized Diego was on his bike, but Dan was sitting on the ground with his head between his knees. He was worse off than me.

"Dan!" Diego yelled.

Grandma and I stopped by him. "You okay?" Grandma asked.

"Yeah," he said. "I hate those things."

"Come on," Grandma said. "Get up. Keep moving."

We helped him stand.

"Thank you," he said.

Grandma gave him a little hug and then we ran-hobbled to the bikes.

Grandma rode in a straight line. I did not ride in a straight line. The crowd was oohing and aahing at my almost crashing and my weaving.

Someone yelled, "Team Stokes!"

Then a bunch of people were doing it. I couldn't believe it.

"Team Stokes!"

"Team Stokes!"

I pushed the fastest speed on the bike and shot ahead. Grandma yelled and caught up. We were going to do this.

At the Jell-O station, there were five huge pans piled with whipped cream.

"I'll find the strawberry," I said to Grandma.

I knew she had spent a lot of time on her makeup that day and plus I'm an excellent swimmer on account of the lake. I can hold my breath forever.

"Are you sure? You almost just threw up."

"I can do it," I said.

She hurried to get the Jell-O.

Diego and Dan pulled up. Dan still looked a little green. It made me like him more, not that I didn't like him before, it just made him seem more normal, is all. I guess UFC fighters are bad at the Tilt-A-Whirl. "I'll get the Jell-O," Dan said. "I'm not eating that stuff."

Diego looked at me. "Good luck."

"Same to you," I said, and I meant it.

Grandma walked over, balancing the pan. "Okay, Meg. Eyes on the prize."

I nodded. My stomach had scaled down. I put my hands behind my back, and I looked over at the crowd, my family,

Dawn Allerton. Silvio Radleaf. This strawberry was all ours.

I took a big breath and smashed my face into the cream and Jell-O.

I moved my face all over the place until I hit something!

I hit something solid!

I came up for air and someone said something, but I didn't hear because I went back down and got the strawberry! I got it!

I got it and everyone screamed.

Dan and Diego looked at me, Diego's face covered in cream.

I had it! They didn't!

Grandma yelped and hugged me. I yelped and hugged her! Cream and Jell-O was everywhere.

We ran to the bikes.

We rode to the Slip 'N Slide. Hoses of water were pouring down the thing.

"Oh my," Grandma said.

"Grandma," I said. "Piece of cake. Let's do this."

I held out my hand. She took it and then we slid on our stomachs to the finish!

53

Freedom!

Grandma and I got first place in the Radleaf Relay and won five thousand dollars for the Alzheimer's Association! That meant we raised six thousand, five hundred and forty dollars for people who had Alzheimer's like Great-Grandpa Jack!

And we got second place overall in the Strawberry Ambassador Competition behind Diego and Dan, who slid in just a few seconds behind us.

That's not too bad coming from last place in the Food Truck Round-Up, even if second is the first losers.

We sat on the stage while Silvio Radleaf awarded Diego and Dan the two bikes of my dreams.

I clapped very hard.

"Thank you, thank you very much," Diego said.

He shook Silvio's hand. Dan did too. Diego smiled at me and I smiled back. They had done a fantastic job. As much as it hurt to say it, they deserved the bikes.

Silvio then said, "We also want to recognize the winners of today's race, Meg and Sally Stokes!"

Everyone cheered. Dad whistled his loudest whistle, Aunt Jenny waved her hat in the air, and Lin was jumping up and down.

I laughed.

"It was a valiant effort," Silvio said, once it quieted a bit.

Then he had us all stand up and take a bow. I hugged Ellie and Cooper and Zoe and Diego. I saved the last hug for Grandma.

"Thank you," I said.

"Like I said, best time of my life." She wiped some cream off my face.

Dawn Allerton went to take back the microphone— probably to tell us it was all over and we could now go buy corn dogs and get on the Tilt-a-Whirl again—but Silvio Radleaf said, "I have one more thing to add if that's alright with you, Dawn."

"Oh," Dawn said, her face turning red. "Of course."

Silvio looked at all of us. Then he said, "I'm just so inspired today. I've decided to donate two hundred electric rental bikes to the town of Jewel," he said.

I gasped! Two hundred rental bikes!

"Not only that, all the participants and their families in this week's competition will have one year of free access to the bikes."

I about fell off my chair.

Lin screamed.

Grandma laughed.

And that's how the Strawberry Ambassador Competition and the War with Grandma ended in victory!

54

Summer Sweetness

That summer was the best summer of my life.

Hattie and I rode rental Leaf bikes to Lin's side of town every single day. We drank frozen lemonades and went swimming and played night games. Mom and Dad rode the bikes on dates and went to the movies and Dad even wrote an essay about the beauty of seeing nature from the road.

I got a job taking flyers around for Jesse Pizza's truck. Jesse even added Meddlesome Meg's Dessert Pizza to his menu and it's one of his bestsellers!

I'm saving up to buy my own Leaf bike next year. Lin is too.

Grandma and Grandpa came to visit and we got to ride around on Leaf bikes to see all Grandma's new friends: Jesse Pizza, Melanie Bacon, Diego and the rest of the contestants;

Silvio Radleaf, who bought a vacation house on the outskirts of town right by Knudsen Strawberry Farms; and of course, Dawn Allerton, who is now Grandma's acting partner! Turns out Dawn is a student of the stage too!

At the end of the summer, we went to see Grandma in the play *The Sound of Music* and when she sang her solo I cried. I really did.

Dad did too. Maybe we all did.

55

For My Readers

This is now the end of my exposé that I hope all the world reads!

It was a long ride, no pun intended, and I hope this is useful to my children and to my children's children and to my children's children's children, because here's the thing, sometimes war with your grandparents is inevitable.

Sometimes you can't stop it.

Sometimes it will control everything you do and think about.

And it's not pretty. Not pretty at all because grand-parents are stronger and weirder and smarter than they look. In fact, here's a list of grandparent characteristics I've compiled to help kids should they find themselves em-broiled in battle.

Stubborn.

Bold instead of old.

Willing to embarrass you and themselves over and over again.

Possibly put produce in cans and rode bikes without shoes when they were your age.

Wear undesirable attire—see clown jumpsuits and tuxedos.

Excellent at picking strawberries and other surprising tasks.

Consume unfortunate foods—see green smoothies.

May upcycle things for reuse—see toilet paper.

Won't give up. I repeat WILL NOT GIVE UP.

Sometimes lonely, just like you.

Know exactly what to say, right when you need it.

And last, but not least, may become the very old and very real friend you never knew you needed.

So beware of grandparents. They're everywhere.

Love you, Grandma Sally.

Love you, Great-Grandpa Jack.

Love you, grandparents of the world.

Sincerely,
Meg Amelia Stokes

ACKNOWLEDGMENTS

Margery Nathanson,
wife of Robert Kimmel Smith

Robert and I would like to thank Ann Dee Ellis for bringing a new generation of readers to *The War with Grandpa*. Ann Dee has been a delightful partner, and it has been a pleasure to get to know her better. We are indebted to John Cusick of Folio Literary Management and Don Laventhall of Harold Ober Associates for introducing us to Ann Dee and helping this project see the light of day. Thank you to the entire team at Delacorte for shepherding Robert's books, especially our editors, Monica Jean and Alison Romig, as well as publisher Beverly Horowitz.

We want to express our gratitude to the many teachers and librarians who brought Robert's books into their classrooms; to his wonderful readers through the past five decades, for their support, affection and encouragement; and finally, to our loving families, our children and grandchildren, who keep us grounded and connected.

Ann Dee Ellis

I'd like to thank first and foremost Robert Kimmel Smith for so many things, but most especially for the world of Peter and Grandpa Jack and now Meg and Grandma Sally. I'm grateful to him and Margery for their support and kindness throughout this process. I'm grateful to my agent, John Cusick, for believing in me and being an advocate and a friend. And I'm grateful to my editors, Monica Jean and Alison Romig, for their guidance.

I also want to thank the dear people in my life who hike mountains with me, walk along lazy rivers with me, and do headstands on the beach with me. I'm grateful for friends who watch my children, read bumpy drafts, and stay up late brainstorming. I'm grateful for parents who believed I could get there and helped me do so. I'm grateful to my little family, who are always my inspiration, always my joy, always my motivation.

And finally, I want to thank grandparents everywhere. Where would we be without you?

Don't miss the prequel!

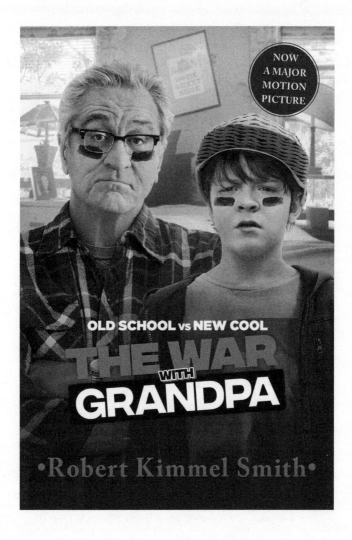

PETER STOKES'S TRUE AND REAL STORY

This is the true and real story of what happened when Grandpa came to live with us and took my room and how I went to war with him and him with me and what happened after that.

I am typing it out on paper without lines on my dad's typewriter because Mrs. Klein, she's my 5th grade English teacher, said that we should write a story about something important that happened to us and to tell it "true and real" and put in words that people said if we can remember and to put quote marks around them and everything.

She also said to keep the sentences short. Looking back on how I began, I can see I'm doing terrible already. The first two sentences took up almost ½ the page.

My little sister, Jennifer, just came in and asked me what I'm doing and I told her. She told me to put Pac-Man in my story and maybe Wonder Woman she watches reruns of every afternoon on Channel 6. "No," I said.

"Why not?"

"Because it is a story about Grandpa and me, silly. Not some made-up thing like on TV."

"Could it have a horse in it?" she asked.

Jennifer loves horses a lot. She cuts pictures of them out of magazines and tacks them up on the wall in her room. "No horses."

"A magic fairy?"

"No!"

"I bet it's going to be a stupid story," she said.

Jennifer was wearing a Pac-Man cap, her Superman T-shirt, a jeans belt that said JEANS on it, and sneakers that said LEFT and RIGHT on the toes. She looked like a walking billboard.

"It is going to be a great story," I said.

"How does it begin?"

"I don't know. That's what I was trying to remember when you came marching in."

"I think it should begin with me," Jenny said, "because I found out Grandpa was coming to live here before you even knew about it."

"Good idea," I said.

"And put in the story that I am very beautiful with long blond hair and lovely blue eyes."

"I just did."

"Now you'll have a good story," she said.

ABOUT THE AUTHORS

ROBERT KIMMEL SMITH was an award-winning author who wrote several popular books for children, including *Chocolate Fever*; *The War with Grandpa* and its sequel, *The War with Grandma*; *Bobby Baseball*; *Jelly Belly*; *Mostly Michael*; and *The Squeaky Wheel*.

ANN DEE ELLIS teaches as an adjunct creative writing instructor at Brigham Young University and has taught at various writing conferences. She lives in the foothills of Utah, and when she's not writing, she's hanging around with her husband and five energetic children. She is the author of *You May Already Be a Winner* and the coauthor of *The War with Grandma*.